Legends Turned to Ash

By:Faithlyn Leach

Dedication

I would like to give a special thanks to my interior illustrator, Jt Williams, my cover illustrator, Matt Duckett, and my editor Michelle Long. I would also like to thank Mom, Dad, Michael, Branin, John, Jaicia, Gabby, Zach, Nick, Abigail, Carlos, Sharon, and Frankie for being such a phenomenal inspiration for this piece of work. Some of you, I have only known for a short time, but the memories that I have of you will last a lifetime. Thank you for your humor and loving support. You will forever be legends in my dragon eye.

Table of Contents

Prologue

Some say back in the days of dinosaurs, a creature mightier than the Earth itself had arisen. Full of majesty and grace it glided through the skies, fearing nothing. With wings as graceful as the clouds themselves, this creature could fly as far as the eye could see and could reach speeds faster than anyone could imagine. As the years went by, more and more of these miraculous creatures began to appear. They were creatures of all different colors and sizes, some as pale as the moon and others as black as night. These creatures could be found anywhere and in every color from blue to pink, to purple, to green. Nothing on Earth could be more magnificent than these creatures.

Some had slim, strong bodies and others had short, weak ones. Scales covered them from the tip of their nostrils to the end of their long, maneuverable tail. All four of their legs had muscle tone and definition. Not only were they excellent flyers, but amazing runners as well.

However, all things good must come to an end. Destruction came upon the world. Lava sprang from volcanos, the ground began to shake, and stars crashed from the sky onto the land. What was once a paradise had now been reduced to rubble. All life vanished, that is, all except the rulers of the sky, those poor, yet wonderful, creatures. Full of despair, these creatures who had lived without a care in the world were forced to move. They traveled to island after island in search of refuge, but one by one the creatures died off.

There is only so much truth known about these creatures that came to be known as dragons; the rest is a mystery. As the world grew to its modern day, scientists gave up on the idea that dragons even ever existing.

Dragons, creatures once filled with hope and delight, had now become a fantasy and may forever remain one.

Chapter 1

Go Away School

"Lightning

Frightening and terrifying

Fills the sky with fear and awe

Serves as light in the darkness

Obeys no one

Fire

Intense and irrational

Fearless and invincible

Knows no bounds

Consuming everything in sight.

Ice

Cold and heartless

Destructive yet beautiful

Speaks with time itself

Always comes back for more

Destruction

Lightning, Fire, Ice

Elements born never to meet one another

For the Earth will fall to destruction

Each made for itself, each with a selfish desire

Never combine these elements

Lightning, Fire, Ice

With these, the Earth will die."

Ding. Ding. Ding.

"That's the bell. Remember students, you must memorize this poem and write an essay about its meaning by the end of summer for extra credit," Mrs. Froid said.

"Talk about boring," I whispered to my friend as I was packing up the drawing of a dragon I had been working on. "I mean, seriously, I know this is an English class, but we're seniors. So why are we still reading these kid poems? At least we only have one more day left until graduation."

Ciara, my friend, answered me with a more hyped than usual tone, "Yeah, I guess they can be boring to some people, but I find them really fun to read! Besides, you were doodling through the whole period, so why are you complaining? Seriously, what is it with you and dragons? I think you need to know that there is an obvious difference between a hobby and mental illness."

I couldn't help but burst into laughter, and Ciara soon followed with her little giggle. Wiping the few tears of joy from my eyes, I picked up my black backpack and whispered, "What? I really can't help it. They are so magnificent! I would give anything to be one, let alone ride one. I wish they were real. Maybe I should just drop everything and go travel the world in search of them."

Ciara couldn't stop laughing at my obsession with the dragons. "Whisper, I think you need help! Therapy? Psychopath facility? Maybe I should just put you in a straitjacket. Anyway, I really can't wait to graduate, and I'm sure the field trip tomorrow is going to be awesome!"

I almost tripped while walking out the door of our casual looking classroom as she said this. "Oh, I forgot about that! We're going hiking in the Rocky Mountains, right?"

"Yep, I can't wait. It's going to be so fun!" She squealed a bit while speaking, completely forgetting about my dragon problem, which was a good thing. Maybe my obsession with dragons was what made me the odd one out.

Ciara was on the smaller side, and I, being five foot eight, was quite a bit taller. She would change up her hairstyle often, but she had been sticking with the short silver colored hair with purple tips for a long while now. I was curious as to when she would find a permeant hairstyle. No matter the style, though, it looked great on her. She had a habit of wearing brightly colored dresses that flowed in the wind as she walked. I liked to think that her bright colors represented her fun, bright, and bubbly attitude; nothing ever seemed to get her down, at least not for long.

I, on the other hand, had a mood that was quick to change, and my long, brown, straight hair never expressed my character. Occasionally, I would add a small braid on each side of my face to bring some style and personality to my hair, but I wasn't sure it was working. Maybe it was because I was too lazy in the mornings to do much to my hair. Even if I didn't look like it, I always dreamed of adventures. It didn't matter whether I wore a headband, braids, or a crazy style. Being me was good enough. After all, my hair didn't look all bad and my clothing style kind of made up for it. Just the other day I was wearing a maroon shirt with a black leather jacket and jeans.

We trotted through the school gate, excited that the day was finally over, and continued down the road to our neighborhood. It was a good thing that we didn't live too far away because I had no clue how else we would get to school. I had a jeep and a license. My family was still working on fixing it, though, so I couldn't drive. That was ok because I had the opportunity to walk to and from school with Ciara every day. Our side of town was always beautiful this time of year, too. The trees began to burst with color, seeds would fly with the wind, and the flowers sprouted in magnificent pinks, whites, and blues. It was gorgeous. Every time I walked by, I just wanted to find a patch of grass and lay down, enjoying the world around me with the sun's rays massaging my face.

The time came for us to part ways, like we did every day, and head to our own homes. It was a small neighborhood, but even so, it was a decent walk to each of our houses.

"Bye Ciara! See you tomorrow morning," I turned around and yelled as we both began to walk away on the newly redone sidewalk.

"Bye, Whisper," she yelled back, waving with a big grin on her lovable face.

As I continued to walk toward my house, I couldn't help but think about the dragon conversation we'd had earlier. I crossed my arms and put them behind my head. I gazed at the clouds drifting through the calm, blue sky and found myself lost in thought.

I don't get it. How is Ciara always so happy? I mean, I try to be nice and smile all the time, but I usually fail. Good intentions aren't the problem either because I really want to help people out and ask how their day is, but I use the wrong words. It makes me sound like an idiot. I am so grateful that she's my friend. It's weird, everyone at school seems to either ignore me or look away. Am I really that awkward? Sometimes I really don't understand humans.

I entered my small house and went straight to my grey and pink room where my laptop was irresistibly relaxing on my bed. It was about four, so I decided to hop on my bed and watch some anime. What else is a teenager supposed to do? Play outside? Seriously, who does that anymore?

My house was usually quiet since my family didn't get home from their jobs and school until late at night. First, there's my brother. I have never met anyone more annoying than him, but you got to love him. Then, there are my parents. They nag a lot, and when I say a lot, I mean it, but they only want the best for us. Finally, there's the pets: cats, dogs, and an iguana. Yep, I've got to say I have a weird family. I fit in, though, so I think it's all fine.

Was this really the life in store for me? My days filled with useless T.V., going to school, going to more school, then becoming a vet? Where's the adventure in that? At some point, I dozed off. Before I knew it, the morning rays of sunlight sneaked into the room and patted my cheeks.

I got up on my own as usual and put on some jean shorts that came a little higher than my knees. Once I slipped on a baby blue colored shirt, I put on my navy blue converse and started out the door.

"Oh crap, my bag!" I wasn't exactly sure how I could forget about the simplest of items, but that's what I did. Quickly making sure I had the necessary supplies and that nothing had fallen out, I rushed out the door.

On rare occasions like this, I had my hair tied back so I wouldn't get too hot while hiking; don't get me wrong, though, I absolutely hated it. I was in such a rush that I didn't even bother to check the weather. Bad idea.

As I started down the sidewalk, I met up with Ciara, and we were too wrapped up in talking to realize that we had already made it to the school. There was little difference in the surroundings on our way to school, so it was always easy to focus too much on each other.

"Oh cool! Look at those huge white buses. I hope those are ours," I said excitedly to Ciara.

"That would be so awesome! Let's go check it out." Ciara ran over to one of our supervisors and asked them about the buses. Her expression bounced from happy to disappointment to happy again.

"I really wish I knew what they were saying," I mumbled to myself. In the blink of an eye, I noticed her hopping back toward me.

"So, are the buses for us?" I asked.

"Nope," she replied with a smile. "Apparently, they are for the freshman trip. Instead of buses, we get to ride with the teachers in the vans. Fun, right?"

I groaned. "You're killing me here."

I glanced over at the line of kids loading into the vans, and with an expression of defeat, I mumbled, "Oh well, can't do anything about it now."

We headed over there and sat in the back of the van. For the whole drive, my mind was lost in thought. The passing trees seemed to hypnotize me.

It didn't take long to make it to the Rocky Mountains, but I was dazed as we walked off the van. Each student was put into different groups, each with different supervisors. Ciara and I happened to get Mr. Jackwell, the P.E. teacher.

Mr. Jackwell was a tall man and had a small ginger beard hanging from his face. "Alright kids, go wherever you want. Just don't get hurt, and we won't have a problem. You aren't babies so you can handle yourselves."

"Hey Ciara, I am going to explore by myself for a bit, ok?" I whispered to Ciara who was surrounded by some of her friends. She nodded, smiled at me, then continued to talk to her friends.

I headed toward the largest mountain and worked my way from there. Each step I took was more difficult than the last. It took some time, but I finally reached the peak of the mountain. I set my bag down beside me and sat down. The mountain faced the town and the people and students below me looked like tiny ants. The sun glistened through the grey clouds as if to stare at the world.

"You know, it's really nice up here," I said to myself, smiling. Below me was a group of students messing around on a ledge. Some of the guys were grabbing sticks, jumping on ledges, and screaming made up words.

"Wish I had a group of friends like that. I bet they are having so much fun." I sighed.

On the other hand, maybe I don't. I don't mind being alone. I should really be used to it by now, plus it gives me time to think about things. I need my personal time. Even if I wanted to have fun with them, I would be facing rejection.

Suddenly, I stopped. "What is…" I questioned myself, noticing a blurred figure in the sky. "Oh, it's heading straight for me!"

My eyes were sealed shut, and I screamed for my life as something tore my body from the ground. Cold scales scratched my arms, and wind that felt like needles rushed into my face.

"Let me down! I don't know who you think you are but this—" I was cut off as my kidnapper dived and spun. "Are you trying to make me yack all over you?" I screamed once more.

"Sorry, my human friend, but I can't put you down. Orders are orders," spoke a low voice with a hint of attitude.

"Seriously! Are you serious? Wait, who just said that?" I asked in frustration.

"Why don't you open your eyes?" the voice said, annoyed.

Slowly, I opened my eyes and tried to tough out the pain of the wind that was rushing into them. I could only see the sky and grey clouds below me. As I glanced above, I screamed, "No! You're…you're…"

"A demon? Monster? Satan himself?" the voice echoed in a burst of laughter.

My eyes were frozen in both shock and overwhelming joy. *A dragon...oh my gosh. A dragon is kidnapping me. This is amazing! I mean, not the kidnapping or hanging thousands of feet in the air part, but dragons exist! Am I dreaming? Wait no, this can't be right.*

"Um, no...you're a... dragon. I can't believe it. A real dragon!" I could barely manage to get the words out of my mouth. Its light blue chest and plated belly were visible above me. I was being held by the dragon's sparkling white arms and legs. They were covered with sharp scales and had claws at the end of each paw. Its front feet held my hands while its back feet held my legs. Based on what I could see, the dragon looked triple my size, not including the wings.

Quickly, the dragon turned its head to look at me. "Well, this isn't so bad, now is it? I had no idea you humans were such fragile creatures!"

"Who the heck are you?" To be honest, I was kind of terrified.

What is going on? Oh, I get it. I must be dead. This obviously isn't real, but if it is what do I do? I mean I don't want her to drop me. I would die.

"Name's Alzora, the last pure ice dragon to exist. What I want to know is who you are, Whisper." Her snobbish attitude remained the same as she glanced at me, annoyed.

"What do you mean who am I? You just said my name. Besides, you mentioned orders. What orders? Where are you taking me?" I asked angrily. We had, obviously, started off on the wrong foot.

She rolled her eyes and set her target on a maze of titanic grey rock formations on the ground. "It will all be explained soon enough."

"What do you—" I couldn't finish my question because something told me that I was already at the destination. Alzora gracefully landed and uncaringly dropped me on the hard dirt floor.

She pointed her head toward a cave entrance and pushed me forward. "Move it!"

"Ow! Ok. Ok. I'm moving, jeez," I mumbled. As we walked forward into the pitch-black cave, I could hear voices further inside. I couldn't tell what was going on, but in the blink of an eye, torches along the sides of a ginormous room lit up. In front of me, a giant black dragon was sitting on the ground looking at his talons and seeming bored.

It was a reasonably flat room, but ledges lined the walls making a sort of staircase. From the outside, nobody would expect the cave to be this large inside. The torches provided a decent amount of light but not enough to see everything in detail, which was kind of creepy. However, the eerie feel of the room didn't compare to the deadly stare the black dragon shot at me.

"Beckett," he growled, "are you sure this human is destined?"

A boy of medium height ran out of a small room connected to the cave. His light green, spiky hair bounced as he stood clumsily beside the black dragon.

Something about him made my heart sink. He wore a light brown cloak with a grey undershirt and a black scarf that fluttered as he walked. His belt was a dark brown and seemed to match perfectly with his brown pants. As he stood in front of the mighty dragon, I could see something move in his scarf. It looked like a long blue tail.

Well, that's weird. I must be seeing things. Then again, I did just enter a room full of creatures that were said not to exist. Maybe I am hallucinating.

Beckett cleared his throat and stuttered, "Ye-yes sir. Everything I have found about her is evidence. Though, I would still like to know what all of this seeking is for."

The dragon growled once more, "Hush boy! If she is not the one, I'm putting you in charge of killing the girl. The world must not learn of our existence."

Beckett glanced over at me for a split second with a worried face but went straight back to his chamber.

"Say what? I am so confused. Will someone please tell me what's happening?" I yelled in an attempt for attention.

"Silence! I am just going to get this over with, so I can go back to sleep. Come here child," he said in a calm, low voice.

"Um…ok," I replied as I walked over to him. He was at least twenty times my size and by far the most massive dragon in the room. Along the walls stood dragons of all colors; all of them were trying to see what was going on.

Yes, that's right, Whisper. Walk over to the 500-ton dragon who probably wants to eat you, because that would totally be a smart choice!

I glanced to the left of me only to see Alzora sitting next to a purple dragon.

"I feel sorry for what sucker is going to have her as their rider. She is way too feisty," Alzora whispered to the dragon next to her. The dragon just rolled his eyes and put his attention back on me.

The mighty black dragon lifted his hand and gently pressed one of his talons against my chest. The cave went pitch black once more, and a blurred vision full of blood, fire, heartache, and destruction raced through my mind.

What in the world was that? Some kind of vision? Well, this just keeps getting weirder. Great. Who were those dragons in my vision? I mean, I couldn't recognize them from the poor quality of the vision, but still, they were rampaging everywhere. Then on the other side of things people, like humans, were screaming and running in circles as their friends and family fell into ravines opening in the ground. Everything was falling apart. Maybe I was hallucinating. Yeah, it must be my imagination. Our world is so peaceful right now. I mean, there have been a couple of earthquakes and stormy nights, but no biggy. That vision was completely different from where I am living right now.

A sick feeling tugged at my chest, and I began to feel light-headed. My head was spinning even more now than it was during my kidnapping. I managed to gather the last of my strength, and what I thought to be sanity, as I looked at my hand in shock. I could hear muttering that I assumed was coming from the dragons, but I didn't know what to think. From what I could see with my limited vision, a cold, blue glow radiated from the back of my hand, and a shape that I couldn't make out had formed in the center.

I didn't realize that the black dragon had been holding me upright with his other paw. It took more energy than anticipated to lift and turn my head to the crowd of dragons. A single dragon in the middle of the crowd glowed the same way as my hand, and the others backed away from her. Her expression was horrified.

What the heck? I can't feel anything, let alone move any part of my body. Why is that dragon glowing? I don't understand. What is happening here? I kind of want to go home—this place is freaking me out, and I don't feel so good. I can barely keep my eyes open.

I was losing my consciousness, and fast, but there was nothing I could do to stop it. I had no choice but to leave myself in the hands of these potentially dangerous dragons. As if my body gave up before my mind, I faded into unconsciousness. This was different again, though. It wasn't like drifting into my dreams; no, it couldn't be that simple. My body throbbed, and my heart pounded. It wasn't until I felt a piercing sensation in my skull and brain that the consciousness abandoned me, the dragon's words echoing through my soul.

"Alas, the darkness of dragons has arisen once again. The egg cast out so many years ago has grown, grown into a new hatred. New darkness, more powerful than ever before. Can you humans find and destroy it in time, as we failed to do so many ages ago?"

Chapter 2

Confusion at its Peak

"Whisper. Hey, Whisper!"

I opened my eyes to see Ciara staring at me with her big, blue, round eyes.

"Come on, silly. It's almost time to go home," Ciara insisted as she poked my shoulder, which ached for some reason.

What just happened? Where am I? Back on the mountain? How? I thought I was dead. There were a bunch of dragons, too. What in the world? Yep, it's official. I am utterly confused. Oh, hey, let's add insane as well. I am thoroughly confused and completely out of my mind.

"Oh! Sorry, I was taking a nap." I had to make up some excuse, but I guess the one I came up with was a little lame. I could have made up some crazy story, but nope, that would have taken brain power that I didn't feel like giving up.

Ok, so maybe what I told her wasn't the whole truth, but how am I supposed to tell her that I was kidnapped by a dragon, knocked unconscious, and somehow appeared here? I can't even manage to explain that to myself, for crying out loud. I can't tell anyone about this either. If I did, they would think I am even crazier than they already think I am. Plus, if someone started a rumor about seeing a dragon, the

government may check into it. Yeah, no. That's totally not happening. Oh man, it gives me chills thinking of what that dragon would do to me if he found out that I told the entire world about their secret. He already wanted to kill me just because I was human. Or maybe not, I don't know. That guy, Beckett? Yeah, he was human, too, so I don't really know what's going on here.

Ciara helped me up, breaking my train of thought, and smiled once more, "Come on, let's go."

"Isn't it a little too early for us to be leaving?" I asked as Ciara dragged me down the path. I'd swear she was part mountain goat.

"Look at the sky silly," she said pointing up. "The rain kind of ruined our day, but don't worry, it was still really fun!"

I nodded, kind of shocked by the rain. We headed down the mountain, trying not to trip on the rocks below us. I say we, but I actually mean I, because I was the only one who had to focus on not tripping or sliding in the mud.

Mr. Jackwell, who was using his coat as an umbrella, met us at the bottom of the mountain and sighed, "You guys are the last ones. Hurry up and get in the van."

As Ciara and I trotted over to the van, droplets of rain tickled my nose. Slowly, it began to sprinkle, and by the time we both were seated on the van, it was down pouring.

As we drove back to the school, I blabbed to Ciara about homework and other stuff that would shift my mind away from reality. It didn't feel real; nothing felt real, and I was genuinely confused. Was it all a dream? Before I knew it, we were back at the school, and Ciara's mom had picked her up.

I glanced down at my bag hanging from my shoulder and grabbed my umbrella from it. Why I had brought an umbrella, I had no clue. My best guess was that I forgot to take it out the last time it rained. It had been raining the whole ride to the school and didn't look like it was going to let up, at least not any time soon. Quickly, I opened my grey dotted umbrella and headed home. After a long, lonely traipse, I finally entered my neighborhood. Stars were beginning to speckle in the fading sky.

It still doesn't make sense. Dragons exist. It's like a dream come true. Though, I wonder what they were talking about. What did they mean by I'm destined?

Suddenly, every light in the neighborhood clicked off, and I was standing face to face with a dark figure. At least, I thought it was a figure; it looked more like a blob of black mist.

"Huh, why the heck would those traitorous worms choose you? Whatever. You will die with the rest of them soon enough," a deep voice spoke, then faded into the night.

Chills ran down my spine, and I stood still, eyes wide open, heart racing.

No, no, no, no! What's happening? My perfect life is gone. All I had to worry about was school. Now there is some creepy guy—correction creepy creature mist thing—who wants me dead, and these weird dragons who think I'm some destined person. Man, I seriously don't understand anything! Can this day just be over already?

Taking a deep breath, I closed my eyes and took a step forward, ignoring the voice. At that moment, all the neighborhood lights popped back on as if nothing happened. My head was spinning like a top, and my heart pounded violently inside of my chest.

"Calm down, calm down," I whispered to myself attempting to relieve the pain my brain felt.

Cautiously, I walked along the path that led to my house, searching for that suspicious being. I could have sworn someone was following me, but each time I turned around, nothing was there. At last, I reached the safety of my home and ran inside, locking the door behind me.

I continued to breathe heavily as I leaned my body against the front door. Water dripped from my hair as I slowly closed the umbrella and rubbed freezing arms. My parents were in their room watching a movie, but I had no clue what my brother was up to. I guess it didn't matter for sneaking purposes. Carefully and silently, I rushed into my room, plopped onto my bed, and pressed my face against a pillow, groaning. Quickly rolling over onto my back, I entangled my body in the comforter and sighed.

"So, today, was quite interesting, wasn't it? It started off with a field trip that led to a kidnapping that, then, led to confusion. Oh, and just when I thought it couldn't get any weirder, I meet some crazy mist thing who claims I will die. I am so confused," I said to myself, frustrated. "Though, was that whole kidnapping thing even real? Wasn't I dreaming?"

My train of thought was interrupted when my brother opened my door. My attention quickly turned to him.

"Who are you talking to?" he said.

"No one. Go away!" I yelled.

He shrugged and shut the door as he left.

I closed my eyes hoping to forget everything that happened, but all I managed to do was enter a land of fantasy and dreams.

I woke up the next morning with heavy eyes. The sun peered through the window, and I had almost forgotten about what had happened yesterday. I wanted to fall back asleep and wait for the whole situation to blow over.

Hesitantly, I hopped out of bed and opened my closet door.

"I don't know what to wear," I mumbled to myself.

I ended up putting on some jeans and a long-sleeved grey and pink shirt after ten minutes of debating what to wear.

"At least it's Saturday and school is done and over with," I said to myself with a slightly more positive attitude.

As I stretched, a mark on my hand caught my eye. Yanking my wrist toward me, I screamed, "What the heck is this? I am positive it wasn't there yesterday. Wait, no. Oh, no. Oh, no!"

Frozen in shock, I sat down on the floor and sorted through my memories of yesterday. "It wasn't a dream. How could it not be a dream? This can't be happening! Wait, is this snowflake the shape that I saw when my hand started to glow? What even is it? Oh, and the more important question is: how am I supposed to hide this from everyone? Jeez, I can picture it now! Ciara will walk up to me and ask: hey, what's that on your hand? Is it seriously a tattoo? That's kind of cool. I would have to convince her that it isn't, and I hate tattoos, but then she wouldn't believe me. The rumor would spread across the whole school, and my life would be over."

I stood back up and looked around to make sure nobody noticed me. My door had been closed, but with the stuff that has been happening, I couldn't be sure I was alone. A cold breeze brushed my skin as I glanced over to the window that was now open.

"I didn't open that." I walked over to the window to close it, but a familiar voice froze me in my tracks. I knew I had to turn around, but I seriously dreaded it.

"Hey, what's up, human?" spoke the voice in a light tone.

"You!" I yelled, falling back down to the floor.

In front of me was a dragon resting its front paws on the window from the outside, her eyes pointed at me like daggers. Her great ice blue wings blocked the view of the sun, and her narrow head was tilted toward me. "Oh, come on. Don't you recognize me? No? Let me give you a hint. My name starts with an A."

I sighed and facepalmed, "Yes, I clearly remember who you are. Alzora? Right? Why are you even here?"

She growled a bit under her breath but managed to keep up her seemingly forced light attitude. "Right! Though that's kind of mean to ask why I am here."

Standing up once more I apologized, "Sorry, I'm just confused. Yesterday was weird. First I was kidnapped by you, then I met something that told me I was gonna die. That isn't how most normal teenagers' lives go."

Completely ignoring the death threat, she replied, "Maybe so, but you aren't a normal teenager anymore. You are destined," her face dropped into disappointment, "just like me."

"Ok, slow down. You guys keep calling me destined. Would you please explain to me what that is? And, why do you keep acting like that is a bad thing? I thought being destined was a good thing?" I asked, frustrated.

"I can't believe no one told you the situation. Beckett was supposed to fill you in, but I guess that fool wasn't up to the task after all. Ok then, I guess if I have to explain I will." She rolled her eyes and took a seat on my soft carpet, her tail still swishing back and forth.

"It all started twenty years ago. I hadn't hatched yet, but I have heard the stories from the elders. It was a time when dragons began to disappear again, but a legend appeared out of nowhere. Don't ask me where or why, because I don't know. It stated that there would be three humans, each bonded to their own dragon. Once these three pairs were gathered, they would save the whole dragon race, but it never stated how. The legend also spoke of an evil force of destruction. Fire. Ice. Lightning. With these the Earth with die. There's a little more to it...something about darkness swallowing the world, but I don't remember that bit. At the time, the elders thought nothing of the legend. When the prophecy of destruction began, though, they changed their minds. Honestly, I don't understand the legend, but whatever, I just do what the elders tell me to. You may not have noticed, but small unnatural phenomena have been occurring all over the planet. So, they started searching for the others who are destined. The problem was that the first destined pair was lightning, then came fire, and now ice. The exact three powers meant to destroy the world. I know you're confused, but you're not the only one! I mean think about it. No one is prepared to hear that they are going to destroy everything and everyone they hold dear."

"Woah, woah, woah, hold up. So, what I'm hearing," I said, trying to make sense of what Alzora was saying, "is that three random humans are mysteriously paired with three random dragons, right? Just because the three pairs happen to represent fire, ice, and lightning doesn't necessarily mean it's us who are going to destroy the world. I mean, maybe there is some other force out there with those elements."

She looked to the side, then glared at me, "Doubt it. There's no way it's a coincidence."

"Well then, how do we know we can believe that legend anyway?"

"We don't have a choice. Weird things are happening to our planet, and that legend is our only lead. We have to give it a shot, at least." Alzora yawned as she rested her head on her paws.

I didn't know what to say. I mean, what would you say in this situation. "I don't care what that legend says. There's no way I would destroy this world. Obviously, that legend has some holes in it. No, I don't believe it at all. I do, however, think that the destined pairs are real and that we may be able to save this planet."

She glared. "You humans are so naïve. You are full of empty words. We have dealt with your kind before. You think you know everything, don't you?"

I couldn't find the words to back myself up because some part of me knew that she may be right. I sighed and looked down at the floor. "What are we going to do?"

"I think Pulri wants us to search for the others," she replied in a more serious tone. "Then, we save my species, and I guess the Earth if we have time."

Talk about a weird sense of humor. Ignoring her last phrase, I was filled with an explosion of confidence. "Yeah! Wait, who's Pulri?"

Alzora giggled. "Oh, he's that big, scary black dragon. He is kind of like our leader, so he acts all tough, but I think he is a nice guy deep inside. He did take in Beckett after all."

"Oh, that guy. Beckett? I remember him. Wasn't he the dorky, green haired boy?" I asked.

"Yep, that was me," spoke a soft and gentle voice. The voice seemed to carry an innocence, of sorts, but also a sense of sadness.

I turned around to find the tall boy staring at me. "Why are you in my room? How!" I screamed. Alzora was just as startled as I was.

"Well, I kind of saw Alzora so I thought I would stop by. By the way, Alzora, I did give Whisper some information beforehand. I made sure that her teacher would give the shortened version of the legend for a writing assignment," he mumbled shyly.

"Oh, well that's nice," I yelled sarcastically. "How was I supposed to know it meant anything? That is beside the point. Haven't either of you heard of knocking? Ugh!" I had no choice but to facepalm.

Knock. Knock. Knock.

"Crap! You guys have to get out of here," I whispered to Beckett and Alzora as I attempted to push them out the window. "What do you want?" I yelled over my shoulder.

"Hey, mom said to make sure your room is clean, so yeah, that's what I'm doing," my brother said in an annoyed voice.

"Can't you do it some other time?" I shouted as I stuffed Beckett into my closet, giving up on pushing him out the window. "Alzora, fly away. Hide? Do something!"

"Who are you talking to?" my brother asked, confused.

Alzora flew out the window the moment I opened the door. "Psh, I wasn't talking to anyone. Nope, not a soul. Just me in here."

He raised an eyebrow and barged into the room. He checked under the bed and glanced at my dressers. "Whatever, I say it's good enough. See ya," and with that, he was out the door.

"Ok, you know what guys? Let's get out of here," I sighed in relief.

Chapter 3

An Adventure?

On my bed was a dark brown backpack full of useful items. I packed necessary hygiene items like a toothbrush, toothpaste, floss, soap, shampoo, and conditioner. I also packed a water bottle, snacks, a small lighter, pocket knife, and some other random stuff.

"Are you done yet?" Alzora asked impatiently. "You humans take such a long time to get ready."

I glanced at her as I was packing the last item. "Could you please stop calling me human? Jeez, I have a name!"

"Ugh, but that's too much work. Whatever. Whisper." She crossed her arms and turned her head to the side, barely glancing at me.

I yanked up the bag and spun around. "Alright, I'm ready! Though, I kind of feel bad running away like this. Isn't my family going to worry?"

"About time, and who cares, they will be fine," Alzora muttered, already halfway through the window.

"Oh, I know I'll leave a note!" I shouted to myself, proud of my idea.

Hey guys, I am heading off for a bit with my friends. I will probably be camping and such, so, don't worry. Alright then, see you soon.

I smiled as I taped the note to my desk. "Ok, Let's go."

Beckett, who had been patiently sitting in one of my chairs, stood up as a sign that he was ready, as well. After both Alzora and I had made it out the window, he followed clumsily.

"It was nice to meet you in person, Whisper. I'm sure we will meet again, soon. Have fun on your journey," Beckett said as he stared at the ground and scratched his head.

"Ni!" shouted a tiny creature popping out of his scarf.

"Oh, hi Dympna. I didn't know you were awake."

"Ni! Ni!" shouted the little creature.

"Woah, what is that?" I asked in awe. The tiny creature, who was about the size of a small cat, climbed on top of Beckett's head and stretched its feathered wings. It reminded me of a miniature fox with a cat-like personality. I had never seen a creature like it before. It had enormous fluffy ears and a little mane around its neck. Its tail was like a cat's, but it was longer, had pink rings around it, and had a ball of fluff at the end. The most unusual part about this creature was its gradient coloration of pink and purple, and that it had two feathered wings on each side of its body, kind of like a dragonfly.

Beckett scratched the little creature's neck and looked me in the eyes. "Her name is Dympna. She is a Vulpeuon, and one of the last of her kind. She's really nice. Do you want to hold her?"

"Wow! She is adorable. Can I really hold her?" I asked excitedly.

Beckett nodded. Carefully, he scooped up Dympna and handed her to me. Her fur was as soft as silk, and I didn't have the words to describe her wings. Remembering our task, I carefully handed her back.

Wow, it's kind of crazy how we really think we know all that there is to this world, but we were so wrong. Dragons exist as well as this little Vulpeuon. There is so much we don't know. I want to learn, though. I want to find out more about their life—the life of a dragon. But first, we need to save the world.

"So Alzora, what did you mean by the destruction has already started?"

Alzora sat on her hind legs and crossed her arms once more. "What I mean is that all our troubles have already begun. When I mentioned that dragons were disappearing, I meant that they would go on a mission or adventure and never return. There was no trace of them once they'd disappeared, but that wasn't the only problem. Pulri has already met up with both the lightning and fire destined before us, and even so, this planet is continuing to rot. If anything, meeting the other destined pairs seems to have sped up the annihilation process. At the moment, the only change we can physically see is the amount of water

30

in the ocean depleting. However, we have been able to sense this impending destruction for quite some time now."

I had no choice but to interrupt. "Wait, so how can the ones destined to save the dragon race also be destined to destroy it? This legend isn't adding up. Besides, we haven't even met the other destined pairs yet, so the elements haven't been combined. We can't be the source of destruction."

Alzora tilted her head and sighed, "You make a good point. All we can do now is wait. Well, wait and try to find the other destined ones. Whatever is going on, we need help, and that's our mission. End of discussion."

I glanced behind me hoping to say goodbye to Beckett, but he was nowhere to be seen. He had left just as mysteriously as he had come. A set of aviation goggles with a note tucked inside sat where he previously stood.

Whisper,

Pulri asked me to give these to you as a…welcoming gift? I hope you like them. Good luck.

Sincerely,

Beckett

"Huh, ok. That was nice of him. So where should we start first?" I smiled as I picked up the goggles and put them on as a headband.

Alzora shook herself from head to tail trying to relax her body and yawned. "Finally! It's about time you are ready to get going! Our first destined one is fire. Pulri told me that he was last seen visiting a small village in New Zealand."

"New Zealand," I shouted, "that's so far away!"

"For once in your life can you stop complaining and just get on?" she mumbled, agitated.

I placed both of my hands on Alzora's lower neck and jumped onto her back.

This really doesn't feel safe. Chills ran up and down my spine.

I tried to calm down my shivers and swallowed hard. "So, any tips on how I am supposed to hang on?"

Alzora opened her wings and glanced back. Her eyes had a devilish look to them, and my face drooped in worry. "Meh, you will figure it out." She smiled. Putting all her power into her back legs, she backed up and shot into the sky.

I screamed like I never had before. Even when Alzora carried me off for the first time, I wasn't this terrified. I was falling backward, so I had no choice but to grab the closest thing to me. My eyes filled with tears as I wrapped my arms tightly around Alzora's neck. I could hear her coughing, maybe choking, but I couldn't loosen my grip.

"Let go!" she yelled. "You're choking me!"

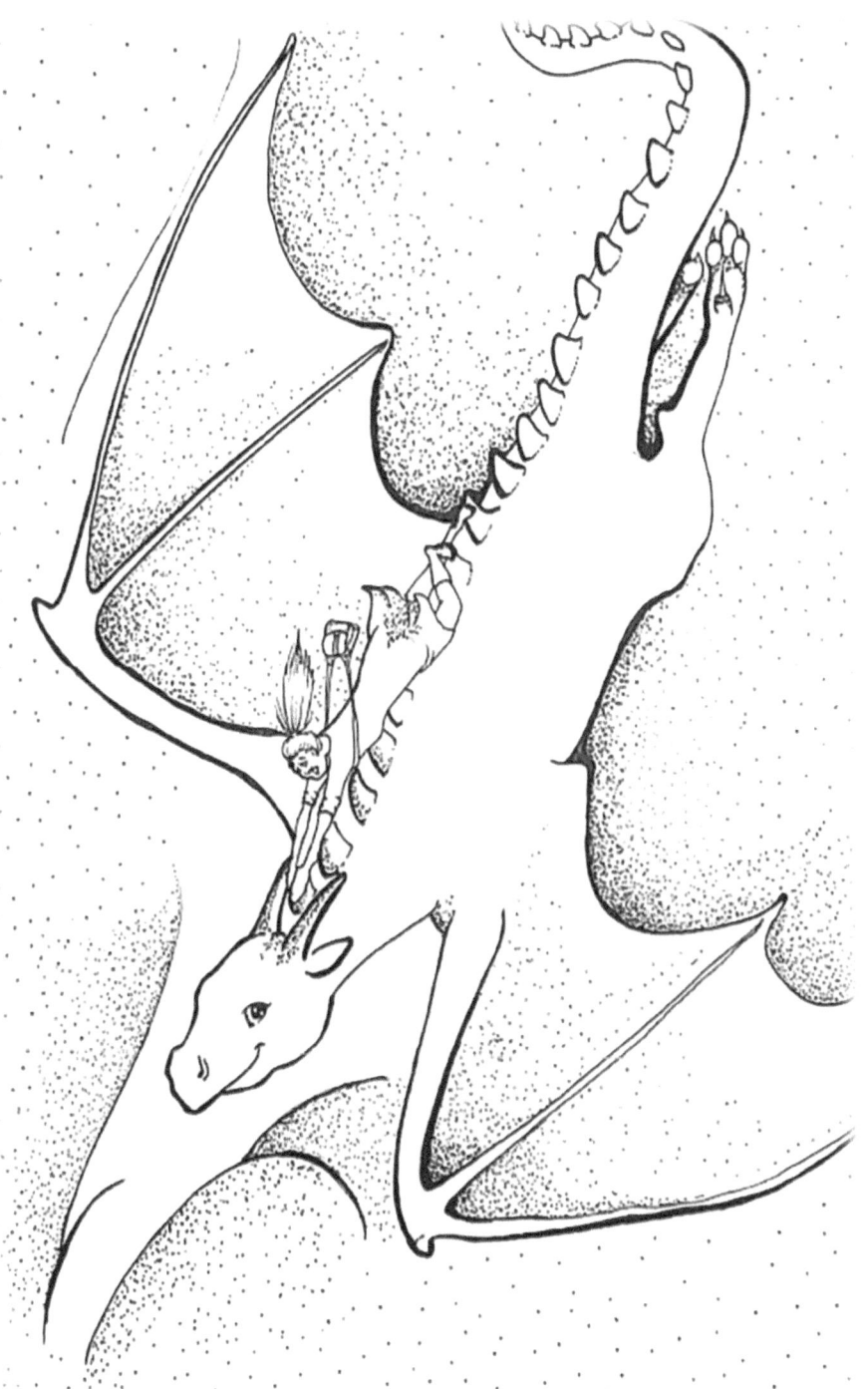

"Slow down! Slow down! Stop flying vertically, or I'm going to fall off!" I screamed back in a panic.

Alzora slowed down and straightened herself out. "What the heck?"

I finally loosened my grip and sighed, "I'm sorry, but I was totally going to die."

"You were going to die? I was the one dying. You were strangling me!" she yelled in astonishment. "I knew you were going to be a thorn in my side."

I tightened my grip on her neck again and smiled deviously. "Not my fault that you don't take care of your guests!"

She bared her teeth. "Oh, so you want to play it that way? You are most definitely not a guest. More like a pest." She flew straight through the clouds above her and then dived in a vertical spin. I screamed even more than I had before. I screamed and screamed, and screamed some more. I screamed until I dared to open my eyes. We were still plummeting, plummeting straight toward the ocean.

"Stop! Stop!" I screamed. "I'm sorry! Just stop!"

No. No. No. No. No. No. I can't get wet! If she dives into the ocean with me, then everything I packed in my bag will get wet, including my phone. Worst yet, I would totally drown. Nope! Nope! Nope! If she doesn't stop... oh, she's going to be in a lot of pain real quick. Then again, not too sure how I could get revenge on a dragon, but whatever, I would figure something out.

During my hurricane of thoughts, Alzora spread her wings at the last second and glided forward at what seemed to be the speed of sound. She was only two inches from the water's surface. I could feel the water that splashed up sprinkling on my skin. With a few short wing beats, she slowed down and rose back into the air. This time, though, I wasn't scared. She was going at a much slower speed. Not too fast, and not too slow. It was perfect. It was comfortable. There was still a hint of terror residing in my body, so I gripped her horns to hold on.

"You know, I'm not as mean as I look. I wasn't going to drench you in water over a little fear," Alzora said calmly. She beat her wings once more in the air.

I smiled and loosened my grip. I moved my hands so that they rested on her neck. "So, how are we going to track this fire dude down? Any ideas?"

Alzora sped up just a little and answered, "Based on what I have been told, I only know that he is in Taupo, one of New Zealand's northern islands. Information about why he is there or what he looks like is unknown."

"That's not much to go off, is it?" I sighed once more.

Alzora sighed as well. "I know."

"How long do you think it is going to take to get there?" I asked, growing slightly impatient.

"Well, considering we will probably stop to rest tonight, I say that we could be there by sundown tomorrow."

"Wow, that's not too long," I replied, surprised. "It's already midday. Time seems to be going by fast. Oh, Alzora, I forgot to ask, but how do you know all these city and country names? I mean, I'm human, and I don't even know where Taupo is."

"Human Geography—by far the worst class I had to take. We even had to do a sky tour above some of the well-known areas," she answered, annoyed.

I cringed at the thought of dragon school. "Yikes, seems like you guys have to learn a lot more in school than we do. But, hey, at least you guys get to explore, right?"

Alzora nodded and put her attention back on the flight. The sun's rays felt good brushing my face. I laid back by habit and let my eyes fall shut.

How did this happen? One minute I am sitting in my room with little plans for the future, and the next I am on a mission to save the world from a mysterious evil power. Correction, a mission to save the world from me. Why me of all people? I'm not special. I don't have many friends or talents, so why? Why me? And why Alzora? I wonder how Ciera is doing. I haven't been in contact with her for a while. I hope she wasn't dragged into this mess like I was. Then again, why would she be? Whatever, next subject. So, Alzora mentioned that the other destined ones are guys. I am definitely in for the trip of a lifetime. A long and possibly irritating trip.

I tried to continue to let my mind drift, but it didn't hold out. I eventually fell into a light sleep. When I felt Alzora land, I woke up. Stars sprinkled the sky and smiled down on us.

"How long was I asleep?" I yawned.

With a straight face, she turned and stated, "Fifty years."

"That long? Hm, how do you look so young?" I exclaimed trying to play along. "So, I'm guessing that we are stopping to sleep, right? And eat?"

Alzora slowly walked over to a large tree and lay down. "Yeah. Though, I am the one who really needs sleep. My wings ache. You were only asleep for a couple of hours by the way. Hope you got your beauty sleep, you lazy human."

"I'm sorry. I know my extra weight probably didn't help the flight either," I mumbled.

She just glared at me and set her head on her paws. I slid off her back and scoped out the area. "Do you think that there is a river nearby? I could catch some fish."

"As if your method of fishing could be any more efficient than mine," she said annoyed.

"I never said my method was better," I replied, confused.

Jeez. She is in a terrible mood. Well, I'll show her!

Before I could say anything, she got up and started walking. "I will get the fish. I know you humans like to cook your food, so build a fire or something."

"Wait!" I shouted, but she was already too far away.

"Well, I guess I can make some beds. That may be useful," I said to myself. "Then, maybe I can make a small fire with my lighter."

I searched around for a bit, looking for something that would be handy, but it was no use. The trees surrounded a large clearing. It was almost like the stars were inviting me to set up camp there. I looked around and sighed. "We have the perfect spot, but there is nothing for me to use to set up. This is a pine forest! In movies, people are always using leaves for beds, but there aren't any. I could dig a hole. No, that wouldn't work. That's it!"

I turned around and stared at the moss resting at the edge of the forest. "Moss. That stuff is perfect for a bed." I rushed over to it and picked up as much moss as my hands could carry. I ran to our campsite and back to the moss. The moss was so soft, and it had a fresh aroma to it. There was a hint of a sickly scent, but the fresh smell seemed to outweigh it.

I continued to get the moss until I thought I had enough. I, first, made an immense pile of moss for Alzora and then spread it out to her size. I made my pile slightly smaller and put it right next to Alzora's.

I stood up quickly, impressed with my work, and smirked. "Yep, this is totally awesome. Such a great idea. Good job, Whisper."

Next, I set up a small campfire area consisting of wood, moss, and pebbles. With two clicks of the lighter, I made a decent fire. It crackled as specs of the red and orange flames scattered into the wind.

Before I could finish praising myself for both the beds and fire, I was nearly knocked over by a rush of wind. Alzora was standing right behind me with fish impaled on each of her front talons. "You were supposed to stay where I left you," she growled in a low voice.

I put on a fake smile and replied calmly, "Yeah, sorry about that. Hey, but look, this place is awesome. We can see the stars, and I even made beds for us! Why are your claws dripping with fish guts?"

Using her teeth, she tore a fish off her claw and threw it right at my face. "Eat."

"Hey!" I shrieked.

I let the fish fall slowly down my face and into my hands. The fish had a glutinous feel to it, and I was disgusted. I had yet to tell Alzora that one of my greatest fears was fish. How could something that tastes so good be so terrifying? Sure, I was ok with eating them, but when it came to touching and holding them, I would lose my mind. Now that I think of it, I don't even know why I offered to help get some fish. My face shifted into an abhorred expression. Alzora must have noticed because she was covering her mouth trying not to laugh.

I threw the fish on the ground, embarrassed. "Stop it! What's so funny?" I could still feel the slime and blood from the fish on my cheek.

Alzora pointed her long, narrow snout upwards and burst into laughter. She was laughing so hard that she fell backward onto the ground. "Your face!"

At this point, my face was blazing with anger and embarrassment, but I decided to stay quiet. Once Alzora was done laughing her head off, she wiped the tears of joy from her eyes and began to shove the fish she caught on her talons into her mouth. All I could her was chomping and the sound of bones crunching. She was eating all the fish! I stared at the fish that I had previously thrown down, terrified. I snatched the fish from the soil, closed my eyes, and took a deep breath. Barely looking at the fish, I cut the head off with a pocketknife, quickly descaled it on both sides, and pierced it with a stick to roast over the fire. After it was slightly burnt on the outside, I carefully plopped myself on the moss bed, and took a big bite out of the side of the fish. It definitely didn't taste like fear. It was delectable.

At last, Alzora raised her head and stretched deeply. She seemed like she was in a better mood now. I honestly thought she was just annoyed because she was hungry. Though, I was kind of annoyed for the same reason.

The moon had risen to the center of the night sky. Alzora crawled over to her moss bed and yawned. I glanced at her once more. On this night, I saw her differently. The full moon in the clear sky shined on her crystal-white scales. Each scale reflected onto the other. Her wings seemed to glow just as the moon did, and her tail spikes absorbed the light. Why didn't I see it before? Alzora was here. She was here, right in front of my eyes. Here on this warm, halcyon night. Here. Here is where I realized that Alzora wasn't on this mission for herself, not even for her dragon comrades. She was here for the human race. The glimmer in her eyes and the relaxed smile on her face told the whole story. She knew that if something happened to the Earth, as it did so many years ago, she would be safe. Dragons were the rulers of the sky, after all. Why was a dragon like her choosing to help humanity?

I put my hands behind my head and rested on my back, gazing at the stars. It all seemed so distant—my life, this mission, and even my friends. Everything seemed so unfamiliar. Here on this night, I had learned one thing. Alzora was chosen to be destined because she had more spirit than any dragon who has ever lived, and if we were going to pull through, we need her to guide us in the right direction.

Chapter 4

A New Friend

My body felt heavy. I was standing, gazing off into the distance. Ahead of me, I could see a dark colored dragon soaring through the sky, panicked. He turned around several times as if something was on his tail, but each time he saw nothing. He was heading for the island directly ahead, an island with a leaking volcano. My vision blurred for a minute, but when it refocused, I immediately noticed these oddly shaped spheres launched from the base of the island. The dragon elegantly dodged the orbs, but to both his and my surprise, an arrow surrounded by a black mist sprung from the earth and pierced his underside. Distracted by the arrow, the dragon yowled in pain. For that one second, he had forgotten about the spheres, and before he knew it, a sphere was right in front of him. It opened and shot out a net that dragged the exhausted dragon back down the to the earth.

My vision blurred once more as I opened my eyes to the early morning sun. *What was that, a dream? It felt so real. Did I witness a dragon kidnapping or a murder? What in the world? Why did it feel so familiar? I know I felt something like that before, but where?*

Attempting to ignore my dream, I put my arms behind my head and stared at the sky. The sun was starting to poke out of the tiny forest clearing. Reflecting on last night, I realized that Alzora had not once tried to put me down on purpose. It was just her way of making jokes, and I had a newfound respect for her. Nobody is perfect, not even dragons, so I tried to avoid her grumpy mood that morning.

"Good morning Alzora." I stretched as much as I could and yawned softly.

"Ehh, morning. Why are you in such a good mood?" Alzora demanded grumpily. She was still trying to make her way out of bed. I didn't think she'd gotten enough sleep. Within an hour of waking up, I was already on Alzora's back and ready to head out. I had no choice but to force a smile and act happy and normal. The only problem was that I ended up seeming weirder than usual. I was lucky that Alzora hadn't caught on. It was frustrating not being able to pinpoint why that dream felt so familiar.

I glanced at her from atop her back. "How much longer do you think it will be?" I needed to focus. I didn't have time to figure out my dream problems.

Alzora unfolded her wings and sprung into the sky, eventually straightening herself out. "I flew a lot longer than expected yesterday, so I think we can be there a little after midday."

"Great. I can't wait to eat at one of the restaurants there. I wonder if they have good food. Oh man, I am getting so hyped!" I threw my hands into the air and laughed with glee.

She rolled her eyes and stared forward, focused on our flight path. "Well that's great and all, but what am I supposed to do? I can't set foot anywhere close to a human."

"Well, maybe you could...no, that wouldn't work. Wait! I think I have extra cash in my wallet. I could probably order you something. Have you ever had human food before?"

Shocked by the question, Alzora smirked. "I don't get how that is even a question. I am a dragon. There is no way I could have ever eaten human food."

I smiled at her. "Well, I don't know! I thought maybe Beckett could have brought you human food."

We both laughed as Alzora ascended higher into the clear blue sky. This moment was so lighthearted. I couldn't help but grin. Everything seemed perfect. It was a moment that allowed me to forget this whole mission and focus on having a good time. It was the best situation for both of us. I knew that both Alzora and I needed to relax and have fun, but it seemed to be an unrealistic idea at the time. I didn't think that we would be able to get to a relaxed point so quickly. It gave me a chance to set this whole dream thing aside for now.

I wished the feeling of relief would have lasted longer because out of nowhere I recalled why my dream was so familiar. *That's it! The dream is just like when Pulri touched me with his talon, and I had that weird vision. Though, this dragon wasn't one of the dragons in the first vision. I don't get it; the visions seem like they are supposed to add up, but I don't think they have anything in common. I guess they both had that black mist, but that brings up a whole other crisis. The black mist resembled the essence that spoke to me that one night when I was walking home. Should I tell Alzora? If I do what would I even say? Oh, hey, I keep getting visions of death, destruction, and kidnappings. You know, the usual. No. I think I will wait a bit. Maybe if I get another vision, I can tell her. I don't have enough information to go off. Plus, it's not like my visions are going to help me right now, anyway.*

Hours passed by, clouds said their hellos and goodbyes, and the wind whistled its tune. It was a little after midday when Alzora shook me from my daydreams and deep thoughts. The flight had consisted of a few dives and spins, but other than that, nothing stood out. It seemed to take forever, but we arrived at last. New Zealand. I remembered that back in sixth grade, I wrote a report on the country, but I never imagined that I would get to visit. Alzora slowly glided over a small town, taking care not to be seen by the villagers.

A long river snaked from the ocean into the village. It seemed to cut the area in two. Trees sat between each house, and it was an overall green place. In the distance, beautiful, lively mountains sprung from the ground. It was extremely charming. Alzora spotted a hill a decent distance from the village and decided to land. As always, she reeled in her wings, dived, and gripped the ground with her talons.

Luscious green grass stretched across the hill, and a small log cabin was at the edge of it. The breeze brushed my face as I took in the view. A faint sound of laughter had broken my train of thought.

I glanced at Alzora, whose ears were now twitching. "Is someone laughing?" I asked.

She tilted her head and pointed north. "Yeah, over there. Go check it out."

"Hey! Why me?" I instinctively replied.

Alzora rolled her eyes, "Do I really need to explain this to you? I am a dragon so if that's a human…"

"Oh yeah, forgot about that. Sorry," I said with a smile.

Attempting to be as stealthy as possible, I tiptoed closer to the laughter. One by one, I saw these brown furry balls of fluff pop up from the grass. They were surrounding and jumping on a boy. He seemed to be fifteen or so. The creatures surrounding him were completely unknown to me. They had long beaks and long legs. Apparently, they were the cause of the boy's laughter.

"What do I do in this kind of situation?" I said out loud.

I took a deep breath and slowly stepped forward waving my hand, "Hi?"

Startled, the young boy shooed the creatures off his belly and nervously stood up. He had a ginormous grin on his face as he took a step forward.

"Hi! My name's Asher! What's yours?" He asked kindly, tilting his head.

I smiled back. His innocence and positive attitude were adorable. I wasn't sure why, but he reminded me of a little kid. "My name is Whisper. What are these things by you?"

Asher glanced down at one of the weird looking creatures. "They are called kiwis, flightless kiwis to be exact. They are a type of bird. They are so cute, aren't they?"

I nodded. "Yes, I have to admit they are quite cute."

At that moment, I noticed an abnormal red mark on the side of Asher's neck.

What's that? I wonder could he be… no, that's too much of a coincidence. But it would make sense since he already lives this far from civilization.

My expression became serious. "What is that on your neck?"

Shocked Asher quickly covered the spot with his hand. "Oh, it's nothing. Never mind that. Do you want anything to drink? I could get you something from my house over there. I never get any visitors."

I lightened my tone to ease the atmosphere and make him feel relaxed. "Yes, please. Could I get some water? You are a very kind young man."

Asher went back to his happy expression. "Thanks! Yep, I'll get you water. Be right back."

With that, Asher sprinted over to the log cabin. Once he entered the house and the door shut behind, him I called for Alzora. "Hey. Weird question, but do you think this kid could be the fire destined?"

"Doubt it. He should have met his partner already, and he should have a mark somewhere on his body. I didn't see either of those." As her tail whipped from side to side, she let out a low growl. "Well, this is stupid. What are we going to do now?"

I starred at the clear sky above. "Actually, I did see something on his neck. He didn't want me to see it, though. It's possible that he does have the mark."

Alzora's dark, narrow pupils gazed into my soul. "Ok. How are you going to check for sure? You know, I could always scare him into telling us." Her face shifted into a malicious smile.

A slight snicker sneaked from my mouth. "Oh, quit it. We aren't going to scare him. I'll ask him straightforward. He seems like a nice boy. What could go wrong?"

Alzora rolled her eyes smiling. "Hmph. Well, this will be entertaining."

"Oh, come on, it won't be that bad," I whispered as she launched into the air and flew away.

The next couple of minutes were filled with me twiddling my thumbs and petting the flightless kiwis. They really were adorable creatures. After a while, Asher came from the house holding some bottled water. He had a same ginormous grin on his face as he did before. It took him a while to walk over to me, but when he did, he offered the bottle of water. I gladly accepted it.

"Here," he said joyfully.

"Thank you," I replied smiling. "Ok, this is going to sound weird, and you probably won't want to answer me, but it is important that I know the truth. That red mark on your neck, what is it and where did it come from?"

Asher was a little more than shocked by the question but continued to put on a smile. "Um, nothing. Sorry, why do you want to know? Why is it important?"

I tried to continue smiling as much as he was, but it was difficult when we were talking on a serious topic. "Please, Asher. I know that you don't know me, but it is vital. Please."

He took a deep breath, closed his eyes, and exhaled. "To be honest, I have no clue what it is or how I got it. It kind of just appeared on my neck a few days ago. Also, I remember having this weird dream. It was a fun dream, but also scary. There were dragons and stuff, too."

I didn't understand the whole dream thing he was talking about, but his memory of the mark seemed to match how I got it. Well, except for the fact that I watched it appear on my hand. "Thanks a bunch. Can I get a closer look at it?"

Asher hesitated, but soon nodded and tilted his head to the side so I could see his neck. The mark was a fire symbol made of reds, oranges, and yellows. Smaller teardrop shaped ovals surrounded the symbol. These ovals looked like they were meant to circle the flame in the center. It all made sense. Everything. His symbol that appeared undoubtedly represented fire just as mine represented ice.

"It's amazing," I whispered with a forced smile, pretending not to know anything about it. "Do you by chance know anything about dragons?"

His eyes lit up at the word. "Dragons? I think they are awesome. I play some video games with them in it."

I put my smile back and attempted to laugh, but both came out forced. *What the heck is going on? He is one of the destined. I'm sure of it! Why doesn't he know anything? Is he trying to hide it from me? No, he looks too innocent to do that. He isn't the lying type. What, then?*

A familiar sound that I knew all too well captured my attention. Wingbeats. What I heard were wingbeats. I peered above expecting to see Alzora. *She is always improvising! Why can't she just let me handle this? Wait, that's not—*

The innocent boy, who was once standing in front of me grinning, was now screaming and running in circles with his arms waving in the air. I had to admit, Alzora was right: this was going to be amusing. Putting the boy's actions aside, I focused on the more serious matter. Something was flying toward us, not Alzora and definitely not

Pulri. Asher continued to scream. It was a girlish scream. Eventually, he fainted and fell to the ground with a THUMP!

This unknown dragon flying toward me sent chills up my spine. My legs wouldn't move. It was as if thousands of needles were piercing them all at once, an unbearable pain. Humid, scorching heat filled the air around me, and my head began to sweat. I could see the blur of Alzora rushing toward me in full defense mode. The dragon was right above me now. Its chest plates looked as if they were leaking flames. At the last second, I felt something collide with my body and fling me to the hard dirt floor.

Chapter 5

Is This Really Happening?

Dirt went in my nose and scattered into my eyes. The heat and dirt continuously stabbed my lungs with millions of daggers and resulted in a moment of uncontrollable coughing. My eyes pried themselves open as I scanned my surroundings. Asher was still sprawled on the fresh green grass where he fainted. Alzora was fixed behind me in a terrifying defense position—teeth barred, wings unfurled, tail whipped out, and eyes so fierce that they could be mistaken for knives.

I deeply inhaled and dragged my arms in front of me to bring myself up. I rose to my feet and looked at the enemy. A dragon stood before me, about the same size as Alzora. The first thing my eyes noticed were his wings, spikes, chest plates, and tail tip. Flames seemed to engulf his wings. Reds, oranges, and yellows shifted downward on each side. His chest plates were the same way. Instead of spikes running down his back, bursts of fire shot out in random places. Flames surrounded the tip of his tail. The rest of his body was coated with obsidian scales, and his horns and claws were a dark silver. His ears were longer than Alzora's, and he had small flames sprouting from his cheeks. Tiny flame-colored squiggles covered his scales. At last, my innocent blue eyes locked with his bloodthirsty, unmerciful golden ones.

It was a silent and petrifying moment. I couldn't help but be curious about why nobody was taking action. I had to break the silence.

"Who are you?" I asked confidently after clearing my throat.

The mysterious dragon growled and inched closer, his tail lashing from side to side. "I should be asking you the same thing!"

His voice was deep and threatening, enough to send chills down my spine.

Before I could speak, Alzora stepped in. "You first!"

Tension filled the air, so I decided to do the talking to prevent a fight from breaking out. "I'm Whisper. The aggressive one over there is Alzora. Your turn, please."

He lowered his guard a bit and sat down. "I am known as Zephyr. What is your purpose on this island?"

"We are trying to find the fire destined pair," I said.

Alzora whacked me with her tail. "You can't tell him that!"

Ignoring her, I continued, "I guess you could say we're the ice destined pair. Do you know anything about this?"

"I guess my assumption was right. You two pathetic worms really are the other destined ones. Asher and I are the fire destined pair, but that imbecile over there doesn't even know that I am his companion. You humans are idiotic. He cannot even look at me without fainting. Then, he wakes up the next morning believing it was just a dream. I thought about eating him more than once! How dare he faint in the presence of such a beautiful, superior dragon," Zephyr snapped.

"Did he just call us pathetic worms?" Alzora twitched in frustration.

It all made sense, the reason why Asher had every sign of a destined one but no memory. I wanted to agree with Zephyr about Asher being a wimp, but I couldn't. He was just an innocent young boy.

"That kind of makes sense," Alzora said easing her defensive position. "Wait, if you had a feeling that we were allies, why did you almost crush Whisper when you were landing? Explain that!"

"That's easy. I didn't care. Plus, if you couldn't save your companion from a dragon simply landing, then neither of you are worthy of being destined. Everybody is alive, so I don't see a problem," Zephyr said with superiority.

"You little…" Alzora nearly lunged at him, but I managed to grab her tail and pull her backward.

Still holding Alzora's tail, I managed to speak. "Well, there is no use looking back on it now. I'm sure we will learn to trust each other soon enough and become friends. I mean, we don't really have a choice now, do we? Though, I think I can help with Asher's fainting problem. If I just explain what's going on and slowly introduce him to you guys, I think he will be fine." I stared at Asher for a moment and then back at Alzora and Zephyr. "Actually, I think I'll go do that right now. Please don't kill each other!"

They locked eyes and growled. Quickly, I ran to Asher's body, which was still lying on the ground. I grabbed the bottled water he gave me earlier and poured a little of it over his face. I wasn't sure if it would wake him up, but it seemed to work. Slowly, his eyes batted open, confused.

I helped him up, and before he could ask any questions, I made my move. "Asher, this is going to sound crazy, but you are not allowed to faint. Ok? Dragons…well, dragons are real. They exist. Apparently, we are destined to save the world and yadda, yadda, yadda. Sometimes details are so overrated. I'll go over them later. Anyway, I have a dragon as a partner and so do you. Mine's name is Alzora, and together we are the ice destined pair. Your dragon's name is Zephyr, and you guys are the fire destined pair. We are going to meet them now. Are you ready?"

The boy seemed speechless, but I guess he wasn't because he managed to blurt out, "Wait. What? That is so cool! This is like a video game. I get to save the world, and I even have a dragon. Awesome! I want to meet them. Come on, let's go."

I was slightly surprised by his reaction, but I had to clarify with him to make sure he was clear on the matter. "You aren't going to faint, right?"

He shook his head and sprung into the air. His glasses bounced right along with him. I sighed, gave a quick chuckle, smiled, and grabbed his hand. "Ok, this way."

As we walked over to Alzora and Zephyr, Asher couldn't keep his mouth shut. "Real dragons! I'm so excited! I wonder if they will like me? Well, hopefully not as a meal. I mean, like a friend."

Anger and tenseness lingered in the atmosphere as Alzora glared at Zephyr with eyes like daggers.

I rolled my eyes at them. "Will you give it a rest?"

The words I spoke snaked in and out of Alzora's long diamond ears, but she did not dare glance at me.

"Hey, I'm serious! Stop it. I don't have time to watch you two glare at each other all day, pondering ideas of how to murder each other and get away with it. Get up and say hi to this kid." It was shocking yet relieving to see that my words had affected them.

Without a word, they snarled at each other and sat in front of the young boy. Alzora seated herself on her hind legs, neatly folded in her wings, wrapped her tail loosely around her body, and let her long front legs vertically descend to the dry dirt. Zephyr, on the other hand, sat on his hind legs, spread out his wings, slashed the air with his flaming tail, and rested his front legs on his knees.

The young boy wore an overjoyed grin and wide eyes. His words were trapped and frozen in awe. With a slow downward movement of the head, Alzora introduced herself. "Hello, Asher, I am Alzora. We have heard much about you. Well, not really. Point is, it is a pleasure to finally meet you, even if your dragon is a spineless coward."

"Says the weakling who would most likely kill her own partner! Anyway, I am Zephyr. I am your dragon for now, but if you dare to show any weakness in battle or attempt to run away, I will find you and kill you. Trust me when I say this, it would not be a quick death. I would tear off your limbs one by one and torch the rest of your pathetic human body." With eyes that held the demons of Hell, Zephyr formed an iniquitous smile.

Nothing could describe the face I wore at that moment. Asher's expression hadn't changed, but he could have been frozen with fear.

"Zephyr. Zephyr! D-did you really say that? What kind of introduction is that? Who does that?" I shouted.

The flaming dragon flicked his tail and grinned once more. "What? I was just being honest. What is the deal with you petty humans? My introduction was far better than that disgrace of an ice dragon. No wonder most of your species went extinct."

His words awakened a side of Alzora that no one had ever witnessed. "What did you just call me? Don't you ever speak of my race! You do not know what happened in the past, or why they all vanished. I will not take this amount of disrespect from an unmannered, ill-willed, immature, childish, naïve, not to mention plain stupid dragon who can't even control the temperature of his flames. I bet you thought no one would notice, didn't you? When it comes to you hot headed dragons, the weak ones who cannot control their fire are banished from the tribe, never to return. You mock everyone else's personal problems, but you should look at your own first. Whisper is a human, which makes her weak already, and she doesn't really even know why she is here. She still moves forward. Asher isn't too bright, but he is here, too, giving this whole thing a chance. I believe you should do the same and stop judging the world."

I wonder if that's why it was so unbelievably hot when he was landing. I mean, it would make sense, but how do I know he wasn't just making it hot on purpose.

Her words settled into me for a moment and surrounded me in a coat of pride. Alzora was right; she always has been. As a weapon, the past can destroy even the mightiest of beings, but as a tool, it can make even the smallest creature move forward. Asher and I understood this fact because it was what was driving us toward our goal.

Zephyr hesitated. Alzora's words had reached him, and there was a chance to start our adventure with a newfound friendship.

It was a long while before anyone spoke, but the first to shatter the silence was Asher. The young boy possessed a smile that could brighten even the darkest of days and shine through the most awkward moments of silence. With this smile and a pure heart, he gazed into Zephyr's eyes and spoke softly. "Hey, I don't care that you can't control your fire. Honestly, I like you the way you are, even if you do judge and threaten people. You are really cool! That being said, please accept me, and let me be your friend."

Asher's words slapped Zephyr at every angle, and for a moment, I caught a glimpse of a tiny smile shift across his face. The smile almost immediately faded, but it was proof that Zephyr was listening and understood what Asher was attempting to say.

"Well, that's that," I stated with a smile, assuming the situation was resolved. "Let's go! Who knows when the next natural, well unnatural, disaster will occur. Plus, we still need to find the lightning guy. We don't have a single lead, and I'm out of ideas. How about you guys start using your heads and come up with a plan."

Alzora stared at me unapprovingly, like always, and spoke at last. "Really? Why would you…why would you want to set off immediately? You even know we don't have a plan, and you want to just fly off into the sunset. Seriously? We just landed! We have— no, I have been flying for days on end! I'm too tired to even think about flying today! That just makes my amazingly intelligent brain hurt. I'm not going."

Zephyr stepped in at this point, as well. "Indeed. I am not going either. I don't feel like it. I am tired as well."

I was pleased by the fact that Zephyr had calmed down and was speaking somewhat politely. On the other hand, I was a tad bit angry at them for not wanting to head out, but I could understand that. It was a bit naïve and ignorant of me for being so obsessed with moving forward, knowing that everyone must have been tired.

"Hey, Whisper. It would be kind of awesome if we had a slumber party at my house. Even the dragons could fit in. Oh, sorry. I mean even

Alzora and Zephyr would be comfortable inside. We have been out here for a long time. It's hot, and I am starving. Please?" Asher's smile was always so innocent, yet so mysterious; I didn't know how to say no to it.

He didn't seem to understand the situation at all, but he continued to follow our plan. He even invited us to rest at his own home. However, I sensed something hidden within him, something that he wouldn't tell us now and might not ever. It was something that only he knew, something of the past and possibly the future. Despite all that, he did make a good point. My stomach had been growling for a while now, and it was so blazingly hot that there wasn't an inch of dry skin on my body.

Thanks, Zephyr, you kind of made it scorching out here. I mean even the green grass is now turning brown. What have I gotten myself into?

As we walked the short distance to his house, exhausted, I noticed that Alzora and Zephyr were proud that they had achieved their goal. They were dead set on relaxing for the rest of the day. As they trotted along, their similarity was apparent. It wasn't clear or understandable, but something about them was so similar. As we approached the house, I realized it was bigger than I had initially thought. The house resembled a log cabin. It was as if it came straight from a picture. The base color of the cabin was a hand brushed grey on maple with small light blue windows placed everywhere. On top sat a matching blue roof that seemed to welcome everyone who came near.

As we approached the sky blue door, a lavender fragrance wrapped itself around me and cleansed my aching brain of all negativity. It was sweet, calming, and charming. Tulips of all colors hung from the porch, and the shadow of a small creature peered at us through the window. Asher hopped over to the door and swung it open with a welcoming smile. Most of the walls inside had a grey base with an accent of blue, and little furniture could be seen. There was a couch in front of the large T.V., and a tall marble table was in the kitchen. As we walked into the house in awe, I caught the full view of the creature in the window. It was a big hermit crab. His body was a light shade of red that shifted into orange then white, and his eyes were a piercing black. His round shell swirled into a gorgeous blue, yellow, black, and green pattern.

I had almost forgotten how great air conditioning was. The minute I stepped through the door, a chill wiggled up and down my spine; it felt like heaven. An embarrassing growl roared from my stomach, and soon other small ones followed. Laughter broke the silence as the day faded into night. Asher may not have had much food to serve, but the food he did make was delicious. He spread ham, turkey, and steak neatly across the table. With each mouthwatering bite, my heart melted.

As we each dragged our bodies to the guest rooms, I couldn't help but be suspicious. Asher was such an innocent kind boy but why was he alone? Why did one person live in such a large house? Where was his family? Before I could finish my one-sided interrogation, I had reached my room. It felt good to flop onto a soft mattress again. The comforters wrapped their soft silk around me and engulfed me in warmth. The deep thoughts I was previously occupied with faded away, and my mind was at ease. Consciousness didn't waste any time leaving my body as I fell deeply into a dreamy wonderland. It was a feeling of pure warmth and innocence that can only be felt in another reality.

In a quick, confusing, and frightening second, the moment of joy and adventure was ripped out my body, and a series of unfamiliar pictures rapidly flipped through my dream world. I saw a swamp, tall trees, and a strange dragon. The images gave me a sinking feeling, but what did it all mean? Toward the end of my strange vision, the dragon appeared reaching out to me, terrified. The detail was vague, but the dragon had a distinguishable shell on its back and as well as large dark blue wings. I wanted to know more, but once again I was torn from my dream world.

"Hey, wake up. I'm bored. It's almost noon, so let's go find that electric guy already. Everyone else is already awake. Wake up!"

There was no doubt it was Alzora who was screaming in my ear. I groaned and rolled onto my stomach, exhausted. "Ok, ok, I'm up."

Still dazed, I hopped out of bed and put on the extra pair of clothes I brought in my bag.

Alzora rolled her eyes, as usual, and stared at me. "You are so slow! Where are we going, anyway? We have no lead."

63

The vision from last night raced through my mind once more, and I understood. I wasn't positive, but the swamp surroundings looked like the Okefenokee Swamp in Georgia. It may have just been a hunch, but at least it was a start.

"Hey, so this may sound a little crazy, but I promise that I'm not crazy. Well, I mean, I am crazy but not this kind of crazy…actually, never mind. Point is, just take my word for it. I saw this strange vision in my dream last night, and part of it was in this swamp I know, or at least I think it was, and there was this dragon in it. Though, he wasn't a normal dragon. He was like mutated or something because he had a huge shell on his back and webbed talons. Honestly, I have no clue why he was in my dream, but he was, so I think we should check it out. By the way, this is probably not the best time to say this, but I have been having visions kind of like this ever since Pulri told me I was destined. Some of them are kind of scary. I don't know what they mean."

Alzora, Zephyr, and Asher all gave me the same look, like I was crazy, but eventually, Alzora spoke out. "Uh huh, so when—"

"Did you say a dragon with a shell?" Zephyr rudely interrupted, ignoring my heartfelt confession.

"Hey!" Alzora thrashed her tail about, attempting to control her frustration and continued, "I was asking a question first. Why are you so idiotic?"

Acting superior as always, Zephyr lifted his snout and puffed out some smoke. "I am obviously more intelligent; therefore, I get to ask the important questions. Anyway, Whisper, did you or did you not say that you saw a turtle shelled dragon?"

Alzora continued to contain her anger and managed to keep her mouth closed for the time being. I, on the other hand, needed to answer Zephyr's question. "Yeah, that's what I said. Why does it matter?"

"Our tribe has been relatively peaceful throughout history, but for such peace to occur, sacrifices must be made. Over the course of centuries, only three dragons were said to have been banished from the tribe. The first was Gedeon. Even in the earliest ages of dragons, measures had to be taken. Gedeon was said to be a dragon created from evil itself due to his dark black and red egg coloration. Typically, an egg of that manner would only be considered unusual, but encrypted on it were the words *'All that lives on this Earth will die by my talons and one other's.'* I don't know all the details as to why the egg appeared that way. I guess our ancestors didn't want to take any chances, so they buried it in a cave 20,000 feet below the island. The second and third cases were more recent. The second case dealt with a dragon born of feather. Few scales covered its body. Such an atrocity was banished from the tribe. The third case was somewhat similar in that we banished a dragon based on his appearance and characteristics. At the time, I believe you humans were having some trouble with power surges, and one of the nuclear power plants happened to explode. The mother of the banished dragon was caught in the explosion and was stranded in the area for several weeks. When she laid her egg, all seemed fine. When the newborn hatched, though, he was mutated. Worried, the mother took her child to the tribe only to find that the dragon must be banished, never to return. They probably thought they would catch whatever disfigurement he had, though I don't think his problem works that way. That dragon had a large shell on his back, webbed talons, and large dark blue wings. He was banished fifteen years ago. If that is indeed the dragon from your dream, then we may have some obstacles ahead of us. Where is this swamp you speak of?"

"You guys are so messed up. I mean, who does that? Talk about discrimination. Seriously. I'm going to have a little chat with your elders when this whole fiasco is over. Ok, the swamp is called Okefenokee. I'm pretty sure it's in Georgia, but I don't know where exactly. It might be near Waycross, but then again it may not be." Sometimes I hated my horrible memory; we covered this information in, like, seventh grade.

I could hear Alzora mumbling to herself in the back, but eventually, she spoke up. "Whatever, I could have told her that. Stop trying to act so superior, you flaming pile of scales. Let's just go already. Let's turn around and head back to the place we started, or at least near there."

Asher hadn't contributed at all to the conversation until now. "Alright, let's go! It's going to be so fun."

I sighed, but at the same time his innocence was amusing. *Part of me feels like these days are going by too quickly, but I don't want our adventure to stop. I mean we haven't done much besides flying a lot and*

meeting Asher and Zephyr. As we argue here, the Earth is still rotting,
oceans are depleting, and I have done nothing to stop it.

Chapter 6

The Mutant and The Psychopath

Soon after midday, we set flight toward our destination. Unsure exactly where we were going, we flew and flew. Clouds passed by, the sun rose and fell, and daydreams persistently tried to pull me from reality. I analyzed everything around me, even the tiniest differences between Zephyr's and Alzora's maneuvers in the sky. Zephyr may be overconfident and arrogant, but he seemed to focus on the path ahead. His movements were filled with strong flaming wing beats as his tail sliced the wind in two. Alzora, on the other hand, tended to close her eyes and enjoy the wind against her scales, sometimes causing her to steer off course. Her demeanor matched her perfectly as she glided through the sky with swift, short wing beats, and a tail surfing behind.

Asher had proven to be an odd boy, to say the least. He was so unsullied and young, yet he maintained a view on the world that no one else would. The chances of him hiding something was high, but the likeliness of it being bad was low. Throughout the flight, he was either fast asleep or passed out from the fear of heights. Either way, he looked peaceful.

Asher was innocent and naïve, yet he was kind and provided us with new perspectives. Zephyr may have been stubborn at times, but he really did mean well and was most likely the most informed in our group. Alzora, the dragon who always seemed to have my back, also seemed to carry a split personality. She could be so optimistic at times and unbelievably pessimistic at others. The one thing that remained the same was her confidence, bravery, and perseverance toward her mission. It may have only been a few weeks since we first met, but I felt like we had been together for years.

My new friends were all so important to me, and I understood how they played a role in our mission. They were all talented and focused individuals who deserved to save this Earth; but, I was not. I was just the average child who attended an average high school. I worked hard to get A's. I doodled in class and hung out with other students.

On the big scale of life, that's all I was to anyone, but on a small scale, life is a little different. I was the weird one who couldn't seem to hit up a conversation right or the klutz who seemed to bump into someone accidentally or mess up a lab. In my regular small town human life, I was just an outcast who managed to make one friend. Other students saw me as that one weird person who sat in front of them in class.

Ciara was my only friend up until now. We would always support each other, hang out, study, and have sleepovers. My life was entirely normal up until that day when Alzora kidnapped me from my field trip. From that point, everything changed. I felt alone and on top of that, I was thrown into a "save the world" situation. I couldn't help but ask what my role was in this big adventure. How could someone with no special qualities or skills be expected to save both the dragons and humankind? I only wanted everyone to be happy and able to fulfill their purpose, but how could I do that if I was just a burden? What could I do to help in this situation?

Then it hit me—there was nothing else I could do except be myself for now. To make our mission work, I had to help as best as I could by being cheerful, even in sad times, and focusing on the frightening visions I continued to have. Maybe if I could do that one little thing, I could fit in with them. Fit in with the only creatures in the world who could save everyone.

I continued to watch the hours fly along with the clouds, passing by in silence. I felt as if an anchor lifted from my shoulders.

Alzora's tail did a quick twitch in the air as she glanced at me. "Hey, what are you thinking about?"

Startled, I uncrossed my hands from behind my head, and with a slow and relieved tone, I answered, "Nothing. Nothing at all."

After a long flight, we had arrived in Georgia, at last. Not knowing where to start, Asher and I split up and headed into the nearest town to find more information on the location of the swamp. Luckily, Alzora and Zephyr found a cave to rest in while we searched the city. There were so many buildings compared to where I grew up. A mixture of shops, skyscrapers, and trees was scattered throughout the city, yet the air was fresh. To my surprise, there were few people on the streets and I was careful as to who I asked about the swamp.

"Excuse me," I said politely to the worker of a small toy shop, "do you possibly know where Okefenokee Swamp is?"

Sadly, he shook his head, "No, sorry. Would you like to buy any of these toys? They just came in today."

I smiled and sighed. "Uh, no, thank you. Thank you for your time, though."

I asked one person after the next, but finding someone who even knew about the swamp, let alone where it was, was impossible. I'd spent a few hours searching when Asher and I happened to bump into each other.

Hopeful, I smiled at him and asked, "So, did you find anything?"

"Oh, dude! They had these delicious caramelized peaches. They were so sweet and salty. I loved them. Oh wait, you probably were asking about the swamp. I asked a couple of different people, and they didn't know. Then, I tried making conversation, but I guess I was talking too much or they had to go or something because they ended up just walking away without a word," he replied happily.

Hm, I wonder if they walked away because of that food you still have all over your face. Wait a minute, since when did you start calling me dude? Oh, Asher, what am I going to do with you?

"Ok, I'm glad you helped yourself to a snack. I wanted to get a snack, but I was a little too focused on our current mission at hand," I mumbled.

Asher tilted his head and looked at me confused. "Huh?"

Clearing my throat, I quickly recovered. "Oh, I was just saying that we haven't really found any information, so I guess we'll have to keep asking. How about her? She seems to like nature."

Simultaneously, we both glanced over to a young girl about eighteen years old with long blond hair sitting on a bench feeding the birds. She was tall, much taller than Asher and I. Even from a good distance away, both Asher and I could tell that she was a very beautiful young lady.

As we walked up to her, she was a bit startled. "Hi, my name's Whisper, and this is Asher. You wouldn't by chance know where Okefenokee Swamp is, would you?"

She blankly blinked twice and shook her head. "No, I'm so sorry. I wish I knew how to help you." I sighed once again, disappointed by our failure.

"Wait," she yelled as we began to walk away, "are you talking about that Wildlife Reservation that just opened up? I mean, I heard that it's a swamp and has a unique name that's kind of hard to pronounce. I don't know if that's the one you're looking for or not, but I thought I might as well let you know."

My eyes jumped wide open and sparkled. "Really, that is so awesome. Do you know where this swamp is?"

She closed her eyes for a minute to think and then opened them. "Yeah, I'm pretty sure if you keep going southeast from here you will reach it. I mean, there should be a sign saying Wildlife Reservation or something, too."

"Oh my gosh, thank you so much. You are such a big help. What's your name by the way?" I asked, excitedly.

She smiled, happy to help and answered, "My name is Adonale. I'm glad I could help. Have fun there. I heard it's really a cool place."

"We will. Thank you Adonale." As Asher and I turned and walked away, we both jumped in the air and high fived. We may not have known for sure if that was the right place, but at least it was a pretty good lead.

It took a couple of minutes to get back to Alzora and Zephyr, but when we did, we had to make the toughest decision of our lives. They were both sleeping. Who was going to wake them up?

"So, who's waking them up?" I asked Asher.

He shrugged, slightly terrified, and held out his hands for Rock Paper Scissors.

I just happened to choose rock as he chose paper. He had trumped me at my own game. "Guess that settles it," he said, snickering. "I'm going to go hide behind that rock."

I whimpered a bit as I tip-toed into the cave, but not a single breath left my body. Once I approached Alzora, I took a deep breath and gently poked her wing. Instantly, her tail twitched and whipped across the ground, tripping me.

"Ow," I whined, accidentally releasing my breath.

Alzora stretched, yawned, and smiled her devious, deadly, sinister smile.

"I'm sorry! We have to leave now, and well, you know. You were kind of asleep, and I had to wake you up," I said frantically as I backed away from her. I had no clue how she was going to react. She was a dragon, after all.

To my surprise, she burst out in laughter, which was even more frightening. "I still can't get over how idiotic and hilarious you humans are. I mean, seriously, what did you think I was going to do? Eat you? Attack you? Well, actually…maybe if I felt like it."

Zephyr, meanwhile, groaned and covered his face with his talons. "Would you keep it down? Some dragons need their beauty sleep!"

Lucky for me, Alzora chimed in this time. "Oh, get up! You don't need any *booty* sleep. So, pick up your fat, arrogant butt, and let's get going."

"What did you say?" He pounced up in anger, flames raging.

I called out to Asher, who was still hiding behind the rock and signaled him to come into the cave. Even as we mounted them and took off into the air, Zephyr and Alzora were still arguing. "Sorry to break up your little cat fight," I yelled, "but if you just head southeast of here for a couple more minutes, we should reach the swamp. I think we just passed a sign."

Alzora listened for the first time in her life and said something somewhat positive. "Amazing, that was quick. I guess you were right after all about the swamp, Whisper."

From that point, it only took thirty minutes to get to the swamp, and once we arrived, I started to regret all the effort I put into finding this place. The swamp was breathtaking, absolutely spectacular. Hundreds of skinny, tall trees rose from the murky green water, and birds flew from the treetops. The only issue was that insects were everywhere. Dragonflies and gnat-like bugs hovered above the water. Beetles and green grasshopper-like insects crawled on the soil beneath us. At first sight of them, I snapped my eyes shut. In my only attempt to open them, I noticed Asher playing with a beetle.

Based on Alzora's attitude, I could tell that she was annoyed with me still on her back. "Get off already!"

With my arms stills wrapped around her and my eyes closed, I refused. "No!"

Astonished she barked back at me, "And why not?"

"Uhh, no reason. I just want to sit here for a bit." At the worst time, a dragonfly landed on my arm, and I screamed bloody murder.

"My ears!" Alzora yelled annoyed.

Zephyr, in the background, chuckled to himself, "Ha! I never would've imagined that a little pest like you would be terrified of insects. It's not like they can do anything except provide me with a decent nutritional snack."

"Stop it!" I yelled with tears of fear forming in my eyes. "Just get it off."

Instead of doing anything, Alzora continued to whine about her ears and subconsciously held them down. Asher, on the other hand, was kind enough to come and help me take the dragonfly off, who at this point was trying to get into my hair.

"There you go little guy," he said as he released it into the wild. "I don't get what you're afraid of. They're cute."

I was positive that I gave him the look of a crazy person. *Cute? Did he just say cute? Well, of course, he would say that. No! No way is anything like that cute. They are ugly, and their only purpose in life is to get caught in people's hair.*

My streak of bad luck continued as I realized the sun was setting and we would have to set up camp for the night. We spent way too much time in the city. If we would have finished earlier, then we may have been able to get in and out of this place before dark. The exact spot we landed in was suitable for camping. It would have been perfect if it weren't for the fact that there were so many insects. It was times like these when I was glad I brought a big blanket to wrap myself in. It would somewhat protect me from the bugs.

We ended up getting ourselves situated in our camping area, and Alzora headed out into the swamp area for a bit. Eventually, she came back in a better mood after catching some swamp fish. I wasn't too sure how safe those fish were to eat, though, or if they were endangered or not. I mean, this was a reservation after all. Then again, the whole Earth was endangered at the time, and Zephyr had roasted the poor fish, anyway. Asher and I quickly devoured the nearly burnt fish, and I laid my blanket across the warm, moist soil.

It was an unusual site for us to camp, so Alzora and Zephyr slept relatively close together to form a "safe" circle for the night. We were all bunched together and ready to fall asleep. No questions asked. I had managed to get a couple of hours of sleep before waking up from another vision. It was from that same dragon as before, the mutant. However, this time he was crying.

What was that? Why am I crying, too? I don't feel sad, so why are these tears rolling down my face? Is he here somewhere? Why else would I have the same vision twice?

Silently, I rose and wandered into the swamp forest with the bright full moon as my guide. The night was so peaceful, yet something about it didn't feel right. After staring at the moon for a while, I realized that I had somehow been turned around.

Well, I'll find them some time. Not a big deal. I always somehow instinctively find my way back. What's that? In the far distance, I caught a glimpse of what looked like neon green eyes staring at me from the water. Well, that's not creepy at all. Ok, so maybe it wasn't a good idea to wander out here alone.

In a split second, whatever had been stalking me sprang from the swamp. Of course, my natural response was to run, so, that's what I did. I ran. I ran and screamed a lot. Based on its shadow, it looked like it could be a dragon, but there was no way I was going to turn around to confirm my suspicion.

"Wait," the creature panted from behind as it chased after me.

Ignoring the mysterious talking, I continued to run until I was out of breath. My heart pounded with each step and nearly burst out of my chest. My legs ran, but they left my mind behind with fearful, restless thoughts.

It's so dark. I can't see a thing out here! For all I know, I am about to fall into the deep, danger-filled swamp water. On top of that, something huge and loud is stalking me and probably wants to eat me or kill me in a horrible agonizing way. I just have to run and keep running! I don't know how long I can keep this up. I'm terrified, and I don't have the mental and physical strength to keep going.

I continued to run with all my strength until I tripped over what felt to be a huge log. "Ow, that hurt," I whined glancing at my leg. A sharp pain jerked through my leg, and a small flow of blood trickled down through my torn pants into the mud. I groaned a little and realized that I wasn't the only one groaning. Hesitantly, I turned my head around to look behind me. There was a lump-like figure on the ground. Startled,

I jumped up, stood still, and ignored the burning pain in my right kneecap. Pinching my eyes closed, I took a deep breath and held it for dear life. In a matter of seconds, I could hear the mud sliding beneath the figure's feet as they frantically rose and stood.

"Who the heck tramples over a guy when he's sleeping!" The deep, loud voice seemed to come from a teenage boy, and he sounded extremely angry.

I blinked for a second, and fled the site once again. The only difference was that the person who was chasing me now was much faster and louder. I could hear him in the distance screaming about how he was going to get me back, or something along those lines. No matter what it was, I didn't plan on letting him catch me.

What is up with this stupid, freaky swamp. First, a wild animal stalks me, now some random weirdo who just happened to be sleeping in the middle a muddy, slippery swamp wants to murder me. Just great! All I wanted was to clear my mind outside for a bit, and this is what happens? It's slippery over here. I am seriously going to slip and fall. That would be kind of bad. Oh man, I am running out of breath, not to mention getting cramps. I just have to keep running.

Fear truly smacked me in the face when I entered a small clearing. The deep swamp water surrounded the clearing and laughed at my helplessness. I was cornered, and with each step, I grew closer toward the water.

Crap! What do I do? There is no way I will go into that water. Who knows what kind of parasites or man-eating creatures live in there. Oh no, here he comes! Maybe I should just start crying. I mean, guys are weak to that right?

As the rampaging teenage boy trampled through the rising swamp trees into the moonlit clearing, I noticed that he wasn't as scary as I originally thought. Don't get me wrong, he was still terrifying, but that was mostly because he was charging toward me with threatening words of murder on his tongue. His outfit reminded me of a ninja's, mostly because of the color scheme and style. His hair was abnormally white and spiky with light blue tips at the end of each strand. It was as if his hair had turned white from electrocution.

Slowly coming to a stop, he threw both of his arms to his side and opened his hands. I thought I was hallucinating, but I wasn't. Tiny blue bolts of electricity were sprouting from his hands, and he smirked at my expression. "Now that I have you where I want you, you are in for a world of pain. Get ready, because I'm gonna…I'm gonna …"

Not even finishing his sentence, or shall I say threat, the mystery boy fell to the ground and started snoring.

I didn't know what to say or even think, so I just stood there. I stood there in that same frozen position and stared at the dangerous, frightening boy who was sleeping right in front of me.

Uh, what did I just witness? Was he sleep-rampaging this whole time? Oh, and what the heck was up with those lightning bolts in his hands. I mean humans can't do that, right?

I was soon broken out of my shocked state when I heard even more crashing through the swamp. This time, what pounced into the moonlight was the turtle dragon. The same turtle dragon that was in my dreams. It was the same exact dragon that was crying, and for some reason, caused me to shed tears as well. There wasn't time to take in any detail because he was charging at me with alarming speed. I noticed that he was trying to stop himself, but the mud was winning. He tripped, rolled, and rolled some more, straight in my direction.

Before I knew what had happened, I felt a jab in my gut and found myself flung into the air, heading straight down into the swamp. I flailed my arms and screamed, disregarding the fact that the dragon was falling as well. With an annoyingly loud splash, we both hit the warm water and came out coughing.

Eeek! What just touched me? Was it a fish? Oh, my gosh! Something is touching my leg, which still stings by the way! What just happened?

Frustrated, I glanced up only to see Alzora staring at me from a tree, laughing uncontrollably. "Oh, I'll give you something to laugh about in a minute!" I mumbled angrily.

Slowly but surely, I made my way back to the clearing and crawled out of the water. There wasn't a single dry, non-muddy part of my body, and I was so done with everything that was going on. Soon after, the turtle dragon dragged his sorry butt up onto the clearing and apologized frantically. I, on the other hand, didn't even bother to stand up and just laid on the muddy earth like a miserable starfish.

Finally getting the chance to take in the dragon's appearance, I noticed that instead of horns he had long fin-looking spikes that traveled all the way down his back and tail, skipping the shell. He had a dark blue body with light blue oval accents and deep purple wings. His chest plates were thick and yellow, and a large brown and green spiky shell covered his back. There were yellow gills on the side of his neck. I didn't have much experience with dragons, but he was definitely interesting looking.

The turtle dragon leaned over me, accidentally dripping even more water on me, and introduced himself. "He-hello. I'm Ugi. I was the one reaching out to you in your dreams. It's kind of a thing I do. Oh, and I should probably mention that it bonds my emotions with yours as well, so sorry about that. Don't worry, though, I can't do it all the time, so it's fine. Also, I'm really sorry I scared you earlier. You run really fast. Did you know that? That human over there is Jaser. He's my buddy. Well, I mean, not really. I'm pretty sure he hates me. I didn't mean to fling you into the water. So sorry about that, too. I really didn't mean to cause you any harm. You are Whisper, right?"

I lifted my head, dropped it back down onto the mud again, and sighed. "Yeah, that's me. You know what, I just don't care anymore. If you will excuse me, I'm going to sleep. Right here, and right now."

As I shifted from consciousness to unconsciousness, I heard Alzora within earshot spouting something abruptly. "So, are you part of our Earth-saving trio? The lightning pair?"

Ugi shifted his webbed talons a bit and glanced at Jaser. "Yes, I guess you could say that. Though, I don't know what to do now. My job was just to lead you to us…"

I smiled and chuckled. *Great. This is just great. Something tells me things are going to start changing on this adventure. Whatever, for now, I am going to sleep. I am going to sleep in the mud just like that crazy human boy over there.*

Chapter 7

Break Time!

As the sun broke from his hiding and rose into the ever-changing sky, he cast heat onto the world. The heat radiated off my skin, turning the once slimy moist mud into a crusty, messy substance. Compared to most of the mornings I have had, this one was particularly bad. I rose from the ground and looked at the sopping wet clothes clinging to my body.

It was so uncomfortable and cold that I felt like crying, but I didn't, of course.

Why am I still wet? This is so not fair. I didn't ask to be chucked into the water like some useless, good for nothing ragdoll! You know what, I'm going to have a little chat with Alzora. I don't care what she says. I'm going to convince her to take me—no Jaser and Asher are coming, too—take us to a town so we can wash up and resupply. The last time I had a proper shower was at Asher's house, and it's been almost a week since then! I didn't even get to wash my clothes there. Alright, that is definitely the plan. Though, I have to wake them up somehow. I'll figure that out in a minute. Maybe I'll just go with it and see how things turn out.

I couldn't help but notice Ugi out of the corner of my eye. He was curled up around Jaser as if he was the most fragile person in the universe. Even as he slept, I could see the sadness written all over Ugi's face.

That reminds me, Ugi isn't like Alzora, or Zephyr, or any dragon for that matter. He didn't even grow up around his own kind. Now that I think about it, he probably grew up around humans since that's who lived around the radiation plant even after it blew up. It's kind of weird how he has a shell. I mean, could it have been a type of radiation mutation? Maybe it was a weird out of place gene? Either way, I feel sorry for him. From what I could see, Jaser probably hates him along with anyone he has ever met, and yet, he still cares for them. He even went out of his way to lead us here through that cool dream power he has. The first time he used it, we were bonded by his fear, and the second time we were bonded by sadness. I want to help him somehow, but I just don't know what to do. I guess I am still a little annoyed that he knocked me into the gross, disgusting, bacteria-filled swamp water, but I can't hate him for that. Ok, I really need to stop thinking so much. I'm wet, and I need a shower. That's all I need to think about right now.

"Alzora, wake up. We're leaving!" I shouted, attempting to sound confident and fierce.

Her ears twitched, her eyes blinked, and her wings burst open. "Aw, that's cute. You're trying to act tough. It's about time you started gaining some confidence. I can't stand having weak friends who can't say what they need to say, right then and there. What's the plan?"

"Friends," The word rang in my head for a moment and then traveled into my heart. It felt good, and for the first time, I realized Alzora did care for me and had developed at least a little respect for me over the weeks we have been together.

I smiled at her and glanced over at Ugi and Jaser who were rubbing their eyes awake. "Alright, here's the plan. Let's go catch up with Zephyr and Asher and head over to the nearest town or city. If we are going to do anything, we need to resupply and definitely take a shower. Don't question it; that's just what's happening! Let's go!"

Jaser, still half asleep, climbed onto Ugi's back with no comment and held on tight as he lifted into the air. I excitedly hopped onto Alzora, as she gracefully pushed herself off the muddy soil in search of the others. It only took a minute or two to spot Zephyr and Asher staring off into the distance. They both seemed hopelessly confused. As we descended to land, Jaser had fully woken up and was shouting questions.

"Where am I? Where did you take me you lil' chicken? Who are those people? Why are there so many dragons? There's like three of them now! Somebody better explain before I kill someone." Unexpectedly, he leaped off Ugi mid-air and perfectly landed next to Asher, who instinctively screamed.

Ugi sighed and smiled embarrassedly as if Jaser's actions were somehow his fault. Jaser took hold of the collar of Asher's jacket and pulled him close.

"Who are you?" he screamed.

With a swift slide of his tail, Zephyr whacked Jaser backward and moved Asher, who was frozen with fear, aside with his talons. "Well if you must know, my name is Zephyr, and that tiny little human is Asher. The real question is who are you?"

Still sitting on Alzora's back in the air, I could hear Jaser's creepy laughter in the distance. Cracking himself up with laughter, he pointed and wiped tears of joy off his eyes. "Hah, your face was priceless! I'm not crazy enough to kill random strangers out of nowhere. I mean, I could, but I don't feel like it right now. You guys are hilarious. Anyway, I'm Jaser, and that chicken over there is Ugi."

He does realize that Ugi is a dragon, right? Why in the world is he calling him a chicken? I'm seriously not too sure what to think about this guy yet. He's either a psychopath or just really dumb.

Silence filled the air as we all blankly stared at him, dumbstruck. As usual, Asher was the first to break the silence, even though he was still a little terrified of the new-found friend. "Where were you? We woke up, and you both were gone. It was kind of worrying."

Alzora smirked and directed her eyes toward me. "This one over here can explain that whole situation."

"It's not a big deal. I just went for a walk and, long story short, I happened to run into Ugi and Jaser. Never mind that, we are heading into the next city to get some supplies and clean up. And, when I say we, I mean you and Jaser, too, because you guys stink. So yeah, let's go. Alzora and I are already set."

"Hey," Jaser interrupted out of nowhere, "why do I have to go? I don't even know you guys."

Ugi swooped down and threw Jaser onto his back as he rose into the air. "Don't worry, I'll explain on the way."

Asher and Zephyr soon followed, and we were back on our never-ending flight path.

A short time had passed, but throughout our flight, we explained the whole situation the Earth and we were in to Jaser. However, his reaction was a little unexpected. "Um, ok. Shouldn't be too hard? Pretty sure I can bash some heads in, right? Like, there's bound to be someone I can fight, right?"

"As long as it's not me," Asher said, quietly.

"Hey, what is with you and fighting people? I mean, you are so obsessed with it that you attempt to attack random people in your sleep," I chimed in.

Asher turned toward me confused. "What exactly happened last night?"

Both Jaser and I coincidently replied with, "Nothing…"

I couldn't help but laugh at last night. "So stupid." Despite still being damp and dirty, I continued to laugh at the stupidity of the scenario.

"Uh, Whisper, now you're doing that creepy laugh, too. Should I be worried about you, as well?" Asher asked concerned.

Alzora joined our little conversation at this point. "Psh, you should always be worried about her! I declared her insane the day we met. Now that we're all together, I may just have to say that you are the sanest of us all, Asher. Then again, I'm pretty awesome and obviously the most intelligent of the group."

"I am not insane!" I argued. "If anyone's insane it's you, Alzora. Plus, you're always picking a fight with Zephyr. It's almost like you're…flirting."

Zephyr glanced back at us slightly alarmed, but before he could say anything, Alzora defended her case. "I…I never…Like I would ever flirt with that heap of charcoal. How dare you even say something like that!"

"Excuse me, pitiful human. What would cause your tiny brain to manufacture that ridiculous idea? I would never even think about flirting with that frozen flying worm. Leave me out of this!" Zephyr stated, holding his snout upward.

From the rear, Ugi cracked up laughing, so much so that Jaser had to lean forward to hang on. Soon after, we all followed. Even Zephyr ended up laughing a little. This was one of those moments that was never meant to end. I wanted to stay like this forever.

This feels good. Even though we have our differences, we all can still have fun together and joke around. I don't want to lose this kind of genuine laughter. It's just too amazing. It means we are all bonded in some way, and I don't mean the legend. We all came together, and we ended up being friends. Sure, we yell at each other sometimes, but we each have some sort of appreciation for one another. Even for Jaser, who I know nothing about. I just know that I appreciate his willingness to be with us right now. The fact that the Earth is eroding as we speak doesn't seem to have phased him at all. That's kind of admirable.

We continued to chat, race, and have all sorts of fun all the way to our destination. When we finally landed, I noticed that the city was more like a small town, but at least it had a motel and a grocery store.

"Where are you guys going to hang out until we are done?" I asked Alzora.

Ugi was the one who ended up replying to my question. "Look! There's a forest over there. If Zephyr can manage not to burn down anything, I think it will provide us with decent cover. Sorry if it's a bad idea."

"I can control my flames just fine! At last, I have managed to get them to obey me," Zephyr growled, annoyed by Ugi's statement.

Alzora just snickered and added, "Yes, that will work fine. Just don't be too long. You know how that makes me feel." There it was, the devious, terrifying smile that I had been waiting for.

Nevertheless, I confidently said, "Yep, we will be back by dusk." Turning to Asher and Jaser, I nudged them and started walking. "Come on guys, let's go!"

We ended up walking into town as a group and received quite a few odd expressions from the townspeople. The town was green all the way around and filled with tons of peach trees. "Ok, there's only one grocery store, so I guess we can split up in there and get some supplies for ourselves. Though, I'm pretty sure there won't be much to buy," I said, trying to take charge.

The three of us stood in front of the store for a second and took in our surroundings.

"Um, question. What are we going to be buying this stuff with? I'm broke." Jaser asked, pulling his empty pockets out of his pants.

Asher sighed, almost as if he were going to say the same exact thing.

"Seriously, guys? I guess I can help out this one time. Just find whatever you need and meet me in the checkout section," I said.

Jaser and Asher smiled and high-fived, then excitedly ran into the store.

Since when did they become best buds? I'm not too sure that Jaser is a good influence on Asher. Hm, let's see. Ok, so after we finish shopping, I can see if the motel here will let us stay in a room for a couple of hours. It shouldn't be too expensive. I wonder if they have a laundry room there because that would be awesome. Oh crap! I better get in there and keep an eye on those two.

The store was even smaller inside than it looked on the outside, but at least it was clean. Quickly, I noticed Jaser and Asher laughing at some toy on another aisle.

Ok, I think I'll grab some extra water, just in case, and some snacks for our flight. These chocolate covered pretzels look really good. I'll just grab a couple. Hm, this rope is like 50% off, but I don't really need it. Then again, who knows. Into the cart you go! Snacks, check. Water, check. Useless item, check. Alright, this looks good. Let's see where those boys are.

It only took a minute for me to spot Jaser and Asher waiting by the first checkout line. They both got snacks, but for some reason, Asher picked up a flash drive as well. I guess he checked the useless item part of the list as well.

"My dude, you have enough to cover this, right?" Asher asked politely.

"Of course she does. She's probably rich!" Jaser interrupted before I could speak.

I rolled my eyes at his stupidity once again. "I'm not rich. I just happened to have some money on my debit card before I came here. I don't know how you guys spent your school year, but I took whatever work I could get to save some money."

Throughout the checkout process, the old, straggly employee was chatting away with a younger employee next to her. "Did you hear about that guy who passed through here?" she asked.

The other employee nodded, and in a low voice he answered, "The one who disappeared at that haunted island?"

The fragile, ancient lady nodded her head as she continued to ring up the supplies. "It's a shame, so many people have been going missing there recently. There's no way I would ever even visit the Atlantic Ocean knowing that that man-eating island is there."

Part of me wanted so badly to ask about the island they were talking about, but I didn't want it to look like I was eavesdropping, even though I kind of was.

As we all walked out the door, I couldn't help but escape into the safety of my own mind.

It's probably nothing, but why would they be talking about an island that's not even near here. If what they said is true, then something is definitely going on. I guess we can check out the area if we find no other leads. Maybe I will get some sort of vision telling us where to go.

Then again, those don't happen too often. I guess there's no use in thinking about this now. I'm so excited to take a shower!

My thought bubble was interrupted when I felt a light tap on my shoulder from Asher. "Where are we going now?"

I smiled, a little embarrassed. "Oh, I'm sorry, I thought I told you guys. We are going to a motel to do some laundry and take a shower. Mostly because we all stink, including me. Actually, I have been wearing deodorant, perfume, and dry shampoo, so I'm probably not too bad. I need a shower because I'm still wet and dirty from when Ugi accidentally pushed me into the swamp."

Asher stared at me blankly for a moment and chuckled. "So that's what happened. I was wondering why you were so dirty. You reminded me of my flightless kiwis from home."

I could only hear Jaser snickering in the distance. "Ha! I wish I would have been there to see that. I guess my chicken can do something right after all."

We continued to walk for a while, talking back and forth until we reached an old looking brown and white motel.

"Is this the place? It's pretty rundown," stated Jaser as he judged the small building.

"It's just until we finish our laundry and all take showers. Oh, by the way, I'm taking one first!" I shouted as I ran into the building.

A well-kempt young lady ran the front and welcomed us in. "How may I help you today?"

"Hi! I was wondering if you had any rooms open just for a few hours. We can't spend the night, but we would really appreciate a room so we can have a shower. We—I have money."

The young women fiddled with the computer for a second and replied. "Alright, one room. Actually, there aren't very many guests this evening, so your timing was great. Do you have any other questions?"

Nervous, I handed her my card and asked my next question. "You wouldn't by chance have a laundry room, would you?"

She smiled once more, and with more typing on the computer, she scanned my card and printed the receipt. "Yes, each load of clothes is about a dollar. I gave you the room right next to it. Please enjoy your stay."

"Thank you!" I grabbed Jaser and Asher who were staring at the Picasso paintings on the wall. "The room's ready."

We headed to our room, and the first thing I did was my laundry. While the laundry was running, I took my nice, warm shower. I could feel the clumps of dirt running off my body as I ran my hands through my hair. Few things in this world could beat the feeling of cleanliness. The moment the water ran onto my knee, I was reminded of the scratch I had somehow managed to get back at the swamp. It was relieving to know that the soap and water were keeping it safe and clean.

Once I finished showering, I brushed my teeth and hair and waited on the bed for my clothes to dry. It was awkward wearing a towel for that long, though. As soon as my clothes were dry, I slipped on my pants and a shirt with a jean jacket. I decided I would wait until the last minute to put on my socks and brown boots. Asher and Jaser didn't bring much laundry, so I washed their clothes together as they showered. I packed my supplies into my bag while dealing with total boredom. It was almost the longest hour of my life. At last, we were ready to leave the motel, and good thing we did, too, because it was already almost dusk. Quickly, I slipped on my aviation goggles as a headband and alerted the boys that we were ready to go.

As we hurried out of the town, we felt a tremor beneath our feet, and I stopped.

Asher stopped as well. "Are you ok?"

Worried I asked, "Did either of you hear or feel that?"

Before they could open their mouths, the ground began to shake and rumble. The once fresh and lively peach trees had fallen to the ground. I could overhear the townspeople screaming and scattering, unsure as to where they should go. We were experiencing an earthquake, but it didn't feel right. Plus, as far as I knew, Georgia wasn't known for tons of crazy earthquakes.

Does this have something to do with the legend? Is this all happening because we finally all met together? I mean, the planet has been eroding, but not nearly to this extent or this often. Until now, I have barely noticed. Is this all our fault?

I didn't have time to focus on thinking; I could barely focus on standing up. "Hurry! We have to get back to Alzora, Ugi, and Zephyr!"

Both Jaser and Asher nodded, and we all booked it toward our friends. Oddly enough, once we reached them, the tremors came to a slow stop.

"Well, that was a weird earthquake. What have you all been up to?" I asked acting like everything was normal.

Alzora was the first to answer. "We learned quite a bit about Ugi and how we are the first dragons he has literally ever seen, other than himself and his mother. We also learned how to give you humans powers, which could be useful. Ugi, believe it or not, had some useful information."

Alzora, please tell me that you didn't threaten him or interrogate him to gain this information.

Zephyr stepped in and touched Asher's mark on the back of his neck with his talon. "First is you, my friend. Now, it may sting a little, but just deal with it." Zephyr closed his eyes and concentrated on Asher.

Asher whined for a second and then looked at Zephyr, confused. "Did it work?"

Zephyr shrugged, "I am uncertain, but close your eyes and envision a fireball in your hand, one that you can control and that cannot harm you."

Asher immediately, excitedly held out his hand and did as Zephyr instructed. First came a spark and slowly but surely a round flame appeared in his hands. Asher's smile filled his face as he opened his eyes to admire the fire. "This is so epic, my dude!"

Biting my lip and smiling, I begged Alzora to do me next. It felt strange when she grabbed my hand. It was as if a surge of power had risen within my body. Clenching my fist, I closed my eyes and envisioned that I was shooting a long burst of "ice fire" from my hands when I opened them. My vision came to life, and I created a small layer of ice on the grass. "Thank you so much Alzora! I could just hug you. Actually…maybe not. But, thank you!"

Alzora smiled, happy to be appreciated, and asked, "Where to now? It's almost dark outside so we should get going."

"Ok, this is an odd request, but can we check out a haunted island in the Atlantic Ocean? I think it's toward Spain. I read something about it in an article," I replied.

Zephyr raised his eyebrows amused, "I do not understand how you find out about such odd places, but I believe there would be no harm in checking it out."

"Well besides wasting time, of course, or risking the Earth destroying itself, or us destroying it," Ugi added, paranoid.

Quickly, we mounted the dragons and headed northeast. It took a few hours to get into the area of our destination, but we ended up sleeping most the time, so the journey went by fast. Below us was the raging Atlantic Ocean, and above us were the roaring winds and storm clouds. The clouds were so grey and dark that it was hard to determine whether it was night or early day. Whatever it was, the atmosphere around us was frightening. "Any idea what island it is?" Alzora shouted against the storm.

"I have no clue." At that moment, I felt light-headed as if I was going to pass out, but I didn't. It was fuzzy, but I could see an island with a pointed mountain in the middle as well as two smaller ones on the sides. My ears rang with the screaming cries of a dragon. With another blink, I was in a building witnessing the torture and murder of a jade colored dragon chained to a wall. A young man stood next to the dragon holding a gun-shaped object that seemed to be sucking a green aura-like substance from the dragon and transferring it to the device.

"You are useless to us now," the man declared, and as he spoke, he shoved a long spear through the dragon's chest. The dragon attempted to pull the spear out as blood seeped through the wound. Buckets of blood poured to the floor as the dragon writhed in agony. "Help," he quietly whimpered. "Please, someone help me. I don't want to die. I have people and dragons to look after." I did everything in my power to move, anything that could get that dragon out that situation, but nothing happened. I remained where I was, my eyes fixed on the miserable dragon. He coughed up a mouthful of blood and drew his last breath. His words echoed in my mind as I shook my head, traumatized. I couldn't make out what he was trying to say.

"Hey! Snap out of it!" Alzora yelled noticing I was pouring my eyes out in what looked to be a blind trance. Raindrops fell onto my face, one after another, and I didn't know what to say. One moment I was watching the excruciating death of a dragon, and the other I was back onto Alzora's back. "Whisper! Talk to us!"

Thunder drummed, and lightning rolled through the sky. The wind almost swept me away with it. "What was that?" I whispered to myself with tears still running down my cheeks.

"What was what?" Alzora asked back.

"I think I just had a vision…a horrible, horrible vision. Someone cruelly tortured and murdered an innocent jade dragon. He stole his power—the power and spirit of a dragon. A human being destroyed a dragon on the island directly in front of us."

As tears blended in with the rain rolling down my face, I continued to shake my head in denial. The rain fell harsher by the second, yet all anyone could do was hover in the air in shock of what they just heard.

Chapter 8

The O.S.I

Drop by drop, rain fell onto everyone's skin, filling the sky with a terrifying, eerie mood. Lightning lit up the area, and thunder crackled in the distance. We remained silent for a long while until Zephyr snapped out of his shock.

"Muroganu. There's no doubt it was him." Zephyr muttered quietly looking downward at the island.

Alzora flattened her ears back as if she knew about the name to a full extent, but she could only answer, "Muroganu, the first dragon to disappear since the strange phenomenon occurrences. That was five years ago."

Wiping the trace of tears from my eyes, I calmed down and joined in. "What are you saying? These phenomena didn't start recently? They have been happening for five years?"

"Five years ago, strange things started happening on this planet, but only dragons, as well as other animals, could sense them. It wasn't until this year that volcanos began to erupt all around the world, and earthquakes started popping up in unusual places. The ocean's depletion is recent as well. I believe most of the severe occurrences began this month." Ugi stated in all seriousness.

Zephyr growled for a second and blew steam from his nostrils. "You are leaving one main factor out of that story, Ugi. Muroganu was the only dragon who truly believed some odd occurrence was happening on Earth. He begged others to follow him and help find the reason for the sudden change in environment, but nobody would believe him. Soon after, he left his family in search of the cause, and when weeks turned to months, his friends began to worry. One after another, dragons left in search of Muroganu, but none returned. Until today, there hasn't been a single trace of where he went. I do not understand why or what you humans needed him for, but it is obvious that whatever happened to Muroganu happened to the others as well. Muroganu the jade dragon, the dragon with a power to control other's will."

"That's sad. All he wanted to do was protect his family and the Earth, and no one even tried to believe him." Asher added quietly.

Jaser stepped in kind of annoyed. "What were you guys doing at the time? Why didn't you help him?"

Ugi put on a confused fake smile and scratched his ear with one talon. "Well, I was banished, so I didn't know about that part. Sorry."

"As for Zephyr and I," Alzora said, ashamed, "we were mid-stage dragonets at the time, so we were constantly exploring the outside world and didn't know what was going on in the tribe. I just wish I would have known…"

I glanced down and then at the island, furious and determined. What exactly happened? What did that man do to him? Why? "We can't just hover here focused on what we didn't do in the past. What matters is what we do here and now! We need to go to that island and find out more. We need to know what the heck we are even supposed to do next. It is bothersome not knowing our next step or where we are going. Even as we speak, the ocean is raging, and the volcano on the island is slowly oozing lava. We have to hurry."

With a nod, we all agreed and flew closer and closer to the island until we came to a sudden stop. Alzora began to take in heavier breaths as if she were exhausted, and so did the other dragons. Before backing away a few feet from the island, they began to hesitantly cough, and wobble in the air.

"Hey, what's wrong? Why can't you get closer? Why are you all coughing?" I asked worriedly.

"I… don't know" Alzora attempted to say through the last of her coughs.

"I assume it has something to do with that strange smell. It is creating some sort of reaction for us," Zephyr spoke, holding back his cough.

Jaser glanced at Ugi and then back at the others. "We still have to get down there!"

"I agree! Is there any way you can get close enough to the island so we can jump off?" I asked Alzora.

Finally catching her breath, she replied, "I think so, but we would have to be holding our breath, and you would have to jump off when we are flying at our top speed right next to the shore. There's no way we can actually hover, let alone land, there."

Startled by the response, Ugi tried to argue against it. "Are you sure this is a good idea? What if something happens to them?"

"They will be fine!" Zephyr intervened. "Let's just go already so we can escape this forsaken land."

As we all adjusted our positions on the dragons to a partially standing, partially kneeling stance, the dragons slowly made their way back toward the island. "Ok, are you ready?" Alzora asked, preparing to reach full speed.

"Let's do it!" Jaser shouted against the howling wind and rain. Alzora, Zephyr, and Ugi rose into the sky and dove toward the island reaching speeds never seen before. The wind and rain pounded against our face as we squinted, trying to spot the sandy shore.

"Ok, on the count of three guys, we jump!" I shouted as loud as I possibly could. "One!"

"Two!" Jaser added with a determined smile.

"Ahhh…Are we sure this is a good idea?" Asher frantically asked.

"Three!" Jaser and I yelled as if we were directing it toward Asher.

Using both my arms and legs, I threw myself off Alzora onto the shore and attempted to cushion my fall by rolling. Jaser soon landed next to me and smiled as if it was a competition.

"Where's Ash—" Before I could finish my question, I could hear Asher's high pitched screaming as he clumsily flew toward me. It looked as if Zephyr had used his tail to fling him off. With a thud and a pain in my side, Asher fell right on top of me, knocking us both to the ground. "Ughh," I moaned, "not again. Why am I the one you people always crash into?"

"Sorry," he moaned back, pitifully.

Jaser snickered behind us, dusted off his hat, and then began walking into the island forest.

"Hey, what do you think you're doing?" I asked, quickly jumping to my feet and catching up to Jaser. "Wait for us!"

He shrugged and continued to walk onward once we caught up with him. As we walked, I dusted the small wet grains of sand off my clothes to the best of my ability. At least when we reached the forest, the trees blocked most of the rain. Rain patted the leaves, frogs croaked within the shadows, and a light fog surrounded us. In the distance, a dark mist shaped a short man with a tiny beard who turned smiled at us. Startled I rubbed my eyes and looked in the direction once more.

Who was that? Am I just seeing things, or was a guy just there, staring at us? This island is way too weird, not to mention evil. He kind of reminded me of…no, it can't be. This place is obviously making me see things.

"Hey, did either of you see a guy standing in front of us?" I asked Jaser and Asher.

"No?" Asher answered politely.

"Hah! See I told you she was crazy," Jaser laughed.

"I'm not crazy. You're crazy." I argued. "Where are you even from?"

"You're right. I am kind of crazy!" He laughed some more and then grew serious. "I'm a traveler, and I like to go places, especially dangerously fun places. One time, I went skating in some weird outdoor metal museum and got struck by lightning. Not too sure how I survived, but I did, and next I knew my hair was white."

Asher tilted his head once more, questioning Jaser's sanity. "How did you find Ugi."

"Oh, Chicken? Yeah, I was crossing that old radiated place trying to find some mutated animals and stuff, and I found him. I like him. He's funny and is afraid of me. That makes it even funnier!"

"There is something seriously wrong with you…" I stated in all seriousness. "Oh, and I keep forgetting to ask, but why do you call Ugi Chicken? He is a dragon, you know."

"Hm, good question. I guess I call him Chicken because that's what I call all inferior animals. Also, there may even be a possibility that he is secretly a talking mutant ninja chicken in disguise."

Obviously, because that would make total sense.

After a couple minutes of walking, we came across a large abandoned building with vines beginning to grow down the sides.

"This is the place where Muroganu was murdered," I said hesitantly.

"Alright, let's go inside," Jaser said casually.

"I want to try something," Asher declared excitedly, trying to hide a smile.

He held out his hands and began to grow a ginormous ball of fire. Once it was the size of his liking, he chucked it at the rusty metal doors, causing a mini explosion with trails of flames on the ground.

"Shh, what were you thinking? What if someone is here?" I whispered, frantically trying to use my newfound ice power to put out the flames.

Jaser laughed and gave Asher a high five. "Nice one man!"

How in the world did I get stuck with these two idiots? Jaser is such a bad influence on little Asher. We have to be quiet! Don't they understand that? Maybe, if we are lucky, no one will be home. Yeah, that makes sense. Why would anyone be here anyway? It looks abandoned.

Noticing that they both already entered the building, I hurried to catch up with them. Dim lights hung on the ceiling of the hall we were in, and pictures of scientists hung on the walls. "This place is creepy," I muttered hunching in fear as I walked.

"Agreed," Asher whispered, terrified.

"No way! You guys are total wimps. If we are lucky, maybe we will see a ghost." Jaser snickered. "What's that over there?"

Freezing in our tracks, both Asher and I hesitated before turning our heads toward the entrance to an open room. All we could see was a tall figure, and that was all it took for us to start screaming our heads off.

"Ghost!" we screamed simultaneously.

Jaser sighed and pointed at the figure who was slowly walking toward us. "No, you morons, it's just some old geezer. Look."

"I can say with certainty that I am not just some ordinary old geezer. My name is Rolland. Yeet! Who do I have the pleasure of meeting this fair morning?"

Relieved that he wasn't truly a ghost, I relaxed and adopted a more cautious behavior.

"I'm Asher, that's Jaser, and there's Whisper," Asher stated smiling as he pointed toward us.

"Hey, what are you doing?" I asked, quickly grabbing his arm and pulling him toward me. "Don't talk to strangers! Didn't your parents ever teach you that?"

He smiled, like he always did, and glanced at the tall white-bearded, bald old man. "Yeah, but he looks like a good guy."

Asher is excessively innocent and trusting. Then again, this man doesn't seem evil. He is smiling and so relaxed in his manner; he almost emits a trusting aura as is. Still, maybe I am paranoid, but there's just something about him that I don't trust. For now, I guess I'll see how things go.

"What brings you young fellows into my home? Can I get you anything? Tea? Water? Cheese and crackers?" Rolland asked quiet and polite. His voice was stronger than I expected, and he was quite agile for his age. He really looked like a nice, healthy old man.

"Yeah, I'll take some cheese and crackers. Oh, and water, too. I'm thirsty, so make it quick old man," Jaser ordered as he walked into the nearest room and sat at a table of his own accord.

"Why are you so rude?" I yelled at Jaser, frustrated by his actions.

"Could I possibly have some water?" Asher asked in the correct, polite way.

Rolland nodded and before heading into the room that I assumed to be the kitchen, he replied with, "Certainly, you all are welcome to sit at the table where your friend is sitting. Yeet!"

"I apologize for Jaser's rudeness. I promise he isn't as bad of a guy as he seems." I said as he walked away.

Why does he keep saying yeet? What does that even mean? Oh well, he's old; I guess I can't hold it against him.

Slowly, Rolland turned around and smiled. "No worries, my young friend."

Once he went into the kitchen and shut the door behind him, Asher and I quickly met up with Jaser and sat down.

"Why do you have to be so rude to everyone you meet?" I asked, staring at Jaser.

He shrugged, and the best answer he could give me was, "Eh, that's just what I do."

Man, he is so rude! Yet at other times, he acts like a decent guy. Though, he does seem to be pretty stupid at most times. Ok, so maybe not stupid, but more like lacking common sense. I never imagined that I would be hanging out in a group like this. A boy with overwhelming innocence and trust. An insane teen who can't hold his tongue and has no filter. Three dragons, who usually could care less about the human race, but are helping because they were prophesized to. Even then, they may not have wanted to help. Pulri probably made them come.

As we waited for Rolland, Jaser and Asher passed the time by talking about guy stuff and video games. I, on the other hand, resided within my mind. At last, Rolland arrived holding a tray containing cheese and crackers and three glasses of water. Carefully, he set it on the table and took a seat.

"So, Rolland, what exactly is this place?" I asked.

"In all honesty, it is the former headquarters for the O.S.I," he answered.

Asher tilted his chair back and crossed his arms behind his head. "The O.S.I? What's that?"

"The Organization of Superior Intelligence is a group of what I like to call discriminators. However, their main goal is to eliminate all dragons on Earth, or so I've heard. I have never actually seen the mythical beasts, but I have read about them. The O.S.I believes that any creature that chooses to feel superior to humanity deserves death. Yeet! The basis of their belief is rooted in their desire always to have full control and power in every situation. At the moment, they are stationed in South Africa...woops. I guess my old age is getting to me. I probably shouldn't be boring you with this information. I don't even know if you are allowed to know about it." Rolland chuckled to himself.

"Wow, it's crazy that groups like that actually exist," I stated, buying time for my next question. "Do you have a restroom that I can use?"

"Indeed, I do. It is down the hall to the right. Yeet! Three doors down." Rolland said as he pointed toward the hall.

As I headed into the hall, I said, "Thank you," and then receded into my mind.

I knew it! I knew there was something up with this place! First the vision, then the creepy feeling, and now the O.S.I. What if they are the whole reason why these phenomena are occurring. Maybe they are trying to draw the dragons out one by one, or maybe they just want to kill humanity. Actually, I think drawing the dragons out is a more realistic plan. I guess it's possible that they have some sort of mechanism that's altering the planet. I have an uneasy feeling that this is the same building where Moroganu was murdered. I need to find that room; maybe there's a clue that factors into this whole ordeal.

I quietly raced through the dark, flickering through maze-like halls trying to find the room that had held such bloodlust. I was stopped in my tracts in front of a staircase leading to the basement. Hesitantly, I tip-toed down the pitch-black stairs. My eyes fixed on the darkness that lay ahead. As I grew closer to the main room, I could see the light of a single wax candle, sitting on a podium in the middle of emptiness. The sickly scent of blood flooded my nostrils, and I was forced to cover my mouth with my hand. My vision raced through my mind once more, reminding me of the first incident in this room. The walls and floor were still stained with blood, and shackles hung on the wall. Other than that, the surrounding area was bare, holding no hints or clues. The smell was nauseating, so much so that I had no choice but to run back upstairs.

That was definitely the room; I could sense it. Why did it smell like blood if no one has used it in five years? Could there still be someone here gathering and torturing dragons? If so, it would make sense for the blood to smell fresh and linger in the humid air. Who? Who could be doing this? Unless...the guy I saw in my vision! He didn't have a beard, but the facial features were similar. It has to be him, Rolland! He said this was his home and he knew about the O.S.I and the dragons. If he is actually a member of that organization, I have to get back to the room and check on Jaser and Asher. They could be in danger. There is no telling what he can do. It all makes sense now. Why didn't I notice this before? I have to hurry!

I ran as fast as I could back to the room, attempting not to get lost. My head twisted and turned in every direction to confirm that I was going in the right direction. What I found when I arrived at the dining room was worrisome. I couldn't see Rolland anywhere, and both Jaser and Asher were passed out on the table. As I moved closer, I noticed that they were sleeping, but why was the real question.

"Wake up!" I whispered as loudly as possible. They continued to snore loudly and not budge a bit.

Repeatedly, I lightly slapped Jaser's face back and forth and flicked him. He must have been in a deep sleep because that didn't even wake him up. I guessed that Rolland put some sort of sleeping drug in the water. It was a good thing I hadn't drank any of it.

Ugh! Darn it! If I had been in here, I could have stopped this. I have to find Rolland before he does anything else. Once again, it's all my fault. I have to get those two out of here, but at the same time, I have to take care of Rolland. I can't let him find out that Alzora and the others are in the vicinity either. What do I do?

Before creating a plan or strategy, I frantically ran through the halls in search of Rolland. I turned corner after corner, but it was as if he vanished. It wasn't until I was caught up in a frantic, heart-pounding search that he appeared behind me.

"So, you think you're some sort of hero? Those incompetent dragons told you that you and those other two are meant to save the world or something, right? What a load of crap. Our spy warned us of your little plan to come and destroy us. Yeet. How foolish can you children be? No matter how hard you try, just know you can't do anything to stop us." He chuckled and smiled smugly as he pointed a strange gun toward me. It was similar to the one in my vision, but this one was white and green with a round base. "I kind of feel sorry for what you are about to do. Then again, maybe not. Yeet!"

I couldn't help but be confused about what he just said. Before I could analyze it, he flipped a switch on the device, and a projected green light smacked my forehead. It didn't hurt, but it made me feel weird.

What happened? It feels like my body is moving, but I can't see anything or even hear anything. Everything is dark, why?

It felt as if the darkness was engulfing me as I slowly began to lose all motivation and joy.

I was right before. I am just a useless part of the team. I wasn't even able to help them when they needed me the most. Now Jaser and Asher are in danger. I didn't want to go on this stupid adventure. I could have just stayed home and lived my simple life. I wish I didn't even meet those dragons. They ruined everything. I hate them.

Uncontrollable darkness was swelling inside my heart, ready to consume my whole existence, but something wasn't right. It felt wrong, my feelings—they felt like a lie. Through the darkness, I caught a glimpse of light in the far distance, and I reached for it. I reached farther and farther until the glimpse turned into a brightness that overtook me.

I...hate...them? Hate? Wait...what am I saying? I would never regret meeting my friends. Not ever! I don't know exactly what's happening, but get out of my head!

With that, I snapped out of the trance I was in. I was in a completely different room. On the wall hung a ginormous screen with a control panel.

Where am I? What did he mean he feels sorry for what I'm about to do? Did I do something? Why do I feel so uneasy, and why is my heart aching? What the heck is going on? What did Rolland do to me? Why can't I remember anything? I remember him pointing the device at me and then nothing. Everything is blank.

I noticed Rolland sneaking out of the room, surprised that I broke through the trance. I yelled, "What did you make me do, Rolland?"

He smiled deviously and answered, "Nothing."

Charging at him, I screamed, "You liar!"

Using my power to harden my leg with ice, I jump-kicked him, knocking him to the floor. "I'm not going to let you hurt my friends!"

I didn't have time to fight him. My goal was to get Asher and Jaser to safety, so I left him where he fell and ran out of there. Fueled by both anger and worry, I rushed to the room where the two were waiting, sleeping on the table. Looking through my bag for something useful, I remembered the rope I bought. I knew it would come in handy. Instead of attempting to drag them the whole way back, I just pulled them to the entrance with the previously destroyed doors one by one. I placed them both on a section of the broken metal door, tied the rope to it, and placed both ends in my hands.

I ran with all my might, but they were heavy; well, Jaser was mainly the heavy one. With each step, my shoes slid in the mud and rain slipped in between the crevasses of my hand, making it difficult to hold the rope.

He's bound to follow us if I don't hurry. It feels like my shoulders are going to fall off and my hands burn, but I need to keep going. We aren't that far from the shore. It may not be the shore we started on, but it has to work. It's so close. I can see the opening. Just a little more, I just need to keep going for a little while longer!

I couldn't hide the fact that I was terrified. Rolland had a device that took control of my mind and almost sent it into complete darkness. If he had the chance, I am certain that he would do it again. Rain pounded against my body like needles as I reached the opening. I had arrived at the shore, but I was at a loss for what to do next. It didn't help that I could hear Rolland shouting, "You can't escape from me!" from behind us as he drew closer.

I know they will be able to hear me. They have to!

"Alzora! Ugi! Zephyr! Please get us out of here!" I bellowed at the top of my lungs.

I could see the trees rattling in the distance. I knew Rolland was getting closer. At the moment I least expected it, they came. They dived in all at once, grabbed us by our arms, and flew toward the next island. We didn't even have the chance to climb on top of their backs. It only took a few minutes to get to the closest landmark, Spain. Once we landed, Jaser and Asher woke up. Alzora, Zephyr, and Ugi bombarded them with questions, but of course, they didn't know the answers because they were asleep the whole time. I, on the other hand, had regained my memory and was horrified at what I had done.

Everything had raced through my mind all at once, and I wished with all my heart that it was just a preventable vision. It was a possibility that I regained my memory because I had reached a specific distance away from that strange device, but realizing what I had done was tearing me apart. I could see myself, standing in front of that large control panel, pressing random keys, and searching through top-secret files.

As I looked up from the keyboard onto the screen, I could see a peaceful mountainous area. Caves were scattered everywhere, and the air was clean and breathtaking. Several dragonets soared the skies, playing with each other. Without any ability to stop my finger from pressing the launch button, the beauty of that land was destroyed. Missiles fell from the sky above, crashing harshly into the middle of the mountains, causing an explosion. I couldn't help but look away in horror.

"I'm so sorry…" I intervened quietly as they began to notice me.

"What could you be sorry about? You got yourself and these morons out of that island alive, so that's a good thing." Alzora smirked.

"No…listen to me Alzora. The dragon village, I think I destroyed it…"

Her face grew grim as she swished her tail back and forth. "What do you mean you destroyed my village? That's impossible. You're just a human."

"I didn't mean to! You see there were these missiles, and they were already set to launch toward the mountains." Quickly, my eyes began to tear up and wouldn't stop once Alzora started talking.

"I knew I couldn't trust you! You idiotic human! How did you manage to annihilate an entire village? Zephyr, Ugi, we are leaving. We need to check on the village. We have no idea how many casualties there could be! I don't have time to put up with your petty excuses."

The others nodded, shot us a few harsh glares, and flew off into the distance leaving us stranded in Spain. "Alzora, wait, let me explain!"

All I could hear was the faded angry shout echo through the raging winds covering the ocean. "No."

Chapter 9

The Divided

I couldn't entirely grasp what had just occurred. It was all a blur through my tears and heartache. The dragons, no our friends, left us here. I understood that part, but as for their rash decision, it just wasn't like them.

I get it. Alzora has quite the temper, but I didn't really expect her to up and leave like that without letting me explain. The others went along with her as well, but they didn't even question her. Maybe they all were just worried. If she took us with them, I could have tried to help, though. Why couldn't I be strong enough to break free from that trance? How worthless can a person be? I can't do this. I can't even look at Jaser and Asher; I'm so ashamed. I don't want to burden them anymore, but I really don't want to leave them. If it's for the best, maybe I really should go. I have no choice!

I ran off toward the nearest town, holding my head down trying to avoid eye contact with Jaser and Asher but I couldn't help looking back at them.

Back at the scene of the incident, Jaser mumbled, "Well, I guess that's it for this adventure. Jeez Whisper. How are you that stupid? Even if the whole thing is a misunderstanding, it gives me an excuse to head into town and get some food!"

Soon Jaser left for town, leaving Asher all alone in the flat green spot where we all split up. He opened his mouth a couple of times as if he was about to speak, but instead, he started wandering aimlessly.

I couldn't bring myself to look at them any longer so I charged and trampled through the trees. My heart pounded with each step, and part of me began to fill with hatred, not only toward myself but Asher and Jaser as well.

How could those fools get tricked that easily? I mean, it wasn't even like they were trying to put up their guard or pick a fight. If they would have just thought about what they were doing before they took Rolland's stupid drugged water, then maybe none of this would have happened. I don't get it! Why does everyone have to be so idiotic? I can't even go back to them now. They all hate me!

I arrived in the city only to turn around and find that I had created a trail of frost as I walked. *Oops. Was that because I'm mad at this whole situation? I wasn't even aware that I was doing that. I can't control myself...not my mind, not even my ice power. My source of anger and agony can't only be due to Jaser and Asher though. Maybe part of it has to do with the fact the dragons, my friends, went back home and had no intention of returning to us. Then again, why would they? If someone that I had just recently met accidentally killed my family and friends, I'm not sure if I would be able to forgive them entirely either. It just proves my idiocracy. There is no way I can go back now, even if I did want to return to those morons.*

Feeling this hatred toward my friends and blaming them for my own mistakes wasn't making feel any better. Instead, it was making me more depressed. "I hate this. I really hate this," I mumbled angrily to myself. Light rain patted my face, mocking my gloomy mood.

Walking through the city in the mental state I was in made it nearly impossible to notice anyone besides myself, but there in front of me stood a girl. She seemed so hopelessly lost and confused, but that didn't stop her from mumbling to herself and trying to find her way. Somehow, my empathy for this girl outweighed every ounce of hatred and sorrow that had overtaken my body.

She looked about my age, was a little shorter than me, and had short curly blonde hair that bounced on her shoulders. With a friendly smile forced onto my face, I walked toward her and asked, "Hey, you ok?"

"Well no, actually. My friends got mad and threw a bit of a fit. They both disappeared into the city, and I have no way of contacting them. Always the special snowflake who gets left behind. Do I know you?" the girl replied.

I laughed and put one hand on my side. "No, you just looked like you needed some help. Could I help you find them? Oh, and what do you mean by special snowflake?"

She smiled and looked up at the sky that was just beginning to clear up. "Yes, please! That would be the best. Special snowflake is what my friends and I call me. I mix up words and sentences sometimes or do silly things, so I think that's how it all started. It's a little late for introductions, but I'm Jae."

"Hah, I guess I forgot, too. My name is Whisper. I like your nickname. It's pretty cool," I said, embarrassed about forgetting to introduce myself. "Is there any specific place you think they could have gone? Did they leave as a pair?"

"I'm not sure if they separated, but they were together when they left. I do know that they went in that direction," she said scratching her head while pointing north.

Jae emitted pure, welcoming energy that relaxed my stressed heart. "Ok, that's a start. Why don't we just head that way? What do your friends look like?"

"I think Sahara is wearing a dark blue long-sleeved shirt, and she has brown hair. Kate had like a white and black long coat on and her hair is black and a little curly today?" She questioned herself.

"Alright, let's start then. Shall we?" I smiled as I lead the way she had pointed.

It's not much to go off, but at least helping Jae will keep my mind off that situation. Maybe she will help me get a flight back home as well because that would be totally awesome. I wonder why her friends ditched her. It sounds strange to me. Then again, I am not one to judge, given my situation.

As we passed everyone in the bustling street, I kept an eye out for any pairs that had any of the features Jae had listed. Dark grey clouds loomed over us and thunder drummed through the sky. People of all sorts quickly walked across the sidewalk as if each one of them were late to an appointment, but we saw no sign of Jae's friends.

"Hey, so what could you have done that was bad enough to drive your friends away?" I asked sincerely.

"I accidentally broke her new phone when I borrowed it." As she admitted her faults, I could feel the regret and remorse in her voice. It almost made me just as depressed.

"How did that happen?" I asked, trying to show as much empathy with my expression as possible. I remembered the first time I broke my new phone, and it was an emotional time. However, looking back on it now, those troubles that I'd had in the past were meaningless.

"Well, I was texting and walking, but someone bumped into me, and I tripped. Little did I know, when the phone and I fell, we would both be cracked. The cold hard cement cracked the phone's new glass screen, and it cracked my dignity in the process." Jae attempted to smile through her pain, but it couldn't fix the way her eyes drooped with sadness.

"If they are mad at you, why in the world are you trying to find them? Aren't they just going to yell at you?" I asked, kind of frustrated.

She smiled and nodded her head as if what I asked was ridiculous. "I don't mind if they yell. I want to find them so I can apologize. I want them to know how sorry I am, and that I would appreciate their forgiveness. I would hate for my years of friendship with them to go down the drain. They know I make mistakes. Everyone does. I guess in my case, that's just another reason they call me a special snowflake."

I was at a loss for words, and as we continued forward, I couldn't think of anything to say. I admired her.

She makes it sound easy. Knowing most girls, her friend probably went crazy after she found out Jae broke her phone, and maybe they ditched her out of anger. Whether they meant to leave the situation like that or not, Jae is still going after them for the sole reason of saving their friendship. She even accepts full responsibility for her actions. It's kind of like my case in a way. Why can't I be that brave? I know, for a fact, that part of me wants to find everyone and apologize, but the other half doesn't want to admit my fault and wants to continue to hold anger toward myself and the others. Why can't I be like her? Doesn't she share the same pain and embarrassment that I do?

I pondered on those thoughts for a long while until Jae finally spoke. "Did you hear about that weird animal spotted in the mountains of Cameroon?"

"No? What was it?" I asked curiously.

She looked off into the distance once more in search of her friends and shot her crystal green eyes back at me. "They don't know. No one knows. Some people were calling it a griffin, some said it was just a huge bird, some said it was a science project, and others debated whether the photo taken was even real. I can't even say for sure what it was, but it did have four legs and feathers. That was enough to get me curious."

I wonder if it's…no it can't be. I mean if it really were that banished feather dragon, it would try to keep itself hidden. Right? If dragons exist here then why can't griffins? Or maybe those people were right; it could have been a fake photo. Though, if it really is that dragon, perhaps he could help us find out what's going on with the O.S.I. South Africa headquarters.

"You seem deep in thought," Jae said in a curious yet friendly way. "Any thoughts on what it could be?"

"Oh…um…I don't know. I kind of like the mystery side of it," I lied.

As we passed several different shops, I noticed two girls inside of a makeup store that resembled Jae's description. "Hey, are those your friends?"

"Oh wow, nice eye! Yep, that's them. Thank you so much for the help. I would have never found them without you. Maybe I will see you again sometime?"

"Yeah, no problem. Good luck!" I yelled as she quickly bolted over to her friends, waving goodbye.

What do I do now? I really want to find Jaser and Asher, but what if they are still mad at me? You know what, no! I am not playing this stupid wimpy game of what I am doing with my life anymore! I don't want to leave and forget this ever happened. Whether it's a fake prophecy or a real one, we six were destined to be together and help save the Earth no matter the cost! Heck, even in the small amount of time I have been in this town, I felt a couple of mini-earthquakes, which isn't normal at all. Not to mention, they are my friends! I can't just go around thinking that I will save my friends if I'm not even willing to go back and make amends. I'm done messing around. I'm just going to find them and apologize to each one of them because you know what? They are my friends, and I refuse to let them go!

My emotions about my friends had been bottled up inside me for too long, and I couldn't stand denying the truth of the matter. Nothing was going to change unless I was willing to apologize like Jae and deal with the consequences of my actions. I searched in and out of the city until dusk, but as the sun began to set, I couldn't help but get the eerie feeling that someone was following me. I turned around several times, but each time I did, fewer people were hustling on the streets.

Well, that's weird. It's barely dusk, so where is everybody? Where am I? This place looks kind of sketchy. Why do I feel like someone is following me? I mean, seriously, I'm even beginning to hear footsteps behind me.

I turned around a couple of times only to see darkness. Not a single light lit the area. Cautiously, I tiptoed forward, continuously glancing behind. As I drew nearer to the edge of the city, I couldn't help but feel uneasy. Even then I couldn't prepare myself for the hair-raising, heart-pounding reaction to a cold hand slapping my shoulder. Like any other normal person who was slapped while walking in pitch darkness, I screamed, and I screamed loud. I screamed until the cold hand on my shoulder shifted over to my mouth, shutting me up. Naturally, I bit his hand and turned to see the culprit, and the truth surprised me. My deadly night stalker was none other than Jaser.

"Did you just bite my hand? Like did you seriously just bite my hand? Who does that? How dare you? Ok, this time I'm serious. I am going to murder you, and I will enjoy it," he whispered furiously.

"Jaser?" I was in shock; I never thought he would even consider joining our group again. "Whoops, sorry. Hey, wait! What did you expect me to do? You could have been anybody! How was I supposed to know?"

He growled and muttered to himself. "Whatever, I can't believe you bit me!"

"Guys! Wait…up!" A familiar panting voice whimpered in the distance. "I'm coming, too!"

"Asher! You're back too!" I couldn't help but run up and hug him.

Alright, now is my chance. This is perfect. We are all together. I have to tell them how sorry I am!

"I'm sorry. Ok? I'm sorry. It was my fault you and Jaser were drugged and for not being strong enough to beat Rolland. Because of that weakness, the dragons are gone, and you guys could have died. For that, I'm sorry. All because I couldn't snap out of it when he used that mind-controlling device on me. Please, please Jaser, Asher, forgive me! I didn't mean for it to happen. I know I'm an idiot for trying to run away, but I just couldn't do it. I couldn't leave you guys because…because you just mean too much to me for me to throw away our friendship just like that!" I shouted as tears welled up in my eyes.

"I forgive you," Asher said in a lighthearted, warm voice. "It's ok; it wasn't entirely your fault. I mean maybe we shouldn't have taken those drinks without thinking. So, I'm sorry, too. I didn't mean to cause you two trouble. I was so afraid that you hated me and that's why you left, so I almost couldn't bring myself to come back. I got some help in making the right decision, though. I missed you guys!"

Even though he was right in front of me, I could barely see him in the darkness. I could only imagine that he was grinning.

Jaser grunted as if he wasn't entirely sure of what to say next. "You morons…what the heck am I supposed to do with you? It's not like I like you or anything. I just came back to rub your failures in your face. But whatever, I guess I'll let you off the hook this time. Fine, I forgive you."

It felt as if the darkness that had been guiding me this whole time had finally disappeared and it felt good. It felt good to make the right choice. "Thank you! You guys are so amazing. I don't know what I would do without you! Speaking of which, what made you come back?"

Asher jumped excitedly in the air and raised his hand. "Oh, oh story time. Me first! Can I please go first?"

I couldn't help but giggle. Things were back to normal; everyone was talking and having fun again.

Jaser shrugged and waved his hands in defeat. "Whatever, your story will just make mine seem all the more amazing!"

"Yay!" Asher said sitting down. "Alright, let's start this from the beginning. Honestly, I thought you guys left me for good, like everyone else I have met. I didn't really know where else to go, so I went into the bustling city. There were so many cool colorful boats on the outskirts of the city, and the hills were so green. They reminded me of home. I'm not really a big fan of crowds, so I decided to hide in a video game shop. It was spectacular! There were games everywhere! Some of the games that were sold there weren't even supposed to be released for another month.

Dudes, I'm telling you, it was such a cool store! I really want to go again sometime."

"That's wonderful, and all, Asher, but was that all that happened? You went to a video game store," I asked, trying to edge him to get to the point.

His eyes sparkled, and his smile grew larger and larger as he began to speak once more. "No, no. There is a lot more to the story! Ok, so there was this kid named Dhaka who happened to be looking at the same game I was. I know you always tell me to not talk to strangers, but he looked really nice. Plus, he was a little younger than me. Do you know how hard it is to find another dude who is a video game nerd like me? I can tell you that it's really hard."

I play video games…I think you just need to ask people Asher.

"Anyways, Dhaka invited me to his hotel to play the game, so I gladly said yes. I guess he was on a field trip, but instead of enjoying the Spain sites, he was more interested in playing games—and with me of all people. I used some of my impressive Spanish to get us to his hotel. I'll admit I was a little rusty on it, but it got us where we needed to be. We beat the whole game within a couple of hours, but I couldn't stop thinking about you guys. Even though the game was fun and we screamed so much with anticipation that it should have covered any other thought, it didn't. I missed you guys. Sure, you guys are scary sometimes, but I have had so much fun over the past few weeks that I don't mind. Dhaka and I talked for a long while, but then something

132

about his last sentence hit me. He told me that if I feel this much grief without you all, then maybe just maybe you guys feel the same way. I didn't care how small the chance was. If there was any sort of chance that you guys were going through the sorrow that I was, then I wanted to come back to you. I wanted to come back and cheer you up because nobody should ever feel like that."

I smiled and set my hands on my lap. "Aw, Asher. You are really awesome, do you know that? By the way, your friend was right. I was feeling the same thing. I'm glad you're back."

"Me too. Oh, I got his gamer ID so we can talk anytime online! I'm so happy I made another friend," he said as he leaned backward.

"Not bad, not bad. I bet my story is better, though!" Jaser declared just as insensitive as ever. "Ok, so it all began with a phone call. See, because I'm cool like that. I rang up my homey Carlosi to see if he was in the area, which he was. He's an old friend, but I can explain his story some other time. I wasn't too sure where I was going. I haven't been here in a while. Luckily, I noticed this guy waving over one of those yellow and black cabs, so I pushed him to the curb and took it. What was I supposed to do? Call over my own cab? Nah! One, that takes way too much work, and two, no one in their right mind would give me a ride."

I face-palmed once more. "Let me get this straight. You pushed a random person and then took his cab for pretty much no reason. Ok, seems like you."

"Hey! No interrupting," Jaser yelled. "As I said, I took his cab to the restaurant. You should try it some time. It's called the La Salgan. They have the best food. I met up with Carlosi and his girlfriend Sharonis there as soon as I could because I was starving. Fun fact— Carlosi is actually from Spain and Sharonis is from the Netherlands, but they visit each other all the time. Last time I had lunch with them, they got mad or at least tried to get mad at me, for eating everything in the restaurant and then accidentally breaking the chef's arm. Carlosi is kind of like Asher in a way. You both are kind and understanding. This time I only ate what they could pay for, which left me a little hungry still, but whatever. I won't deny free food. I kind of told them about our situation, but they kept saying stuff like I wasn't acting myself. Of course, normally I would bash anyone's head in who ditched me like you guys did, but I didn't feel like it. Maybe it meant you people are important to me in some way. Eh, who knows? Point is, I decided that this adventure wasn't over yet and came after you. Not going to lie, you both are total morons."

"Yay! Jaser likes us! I knew some part of him never wanted to really murder us!" Asher celebrated.

"I guess, that's good. I still think he wants to kill us though. Look at those eyes," I whispered, pointing at Jaser's dagger-like pupils.

"You are very much right, Whisper…I do want to kill you, especially for that stunt you pulled earlier. I still can't believe you bit my hand!" Jaser lashed out.

"Oh, come on, I didn't bite you that hard." I tried to let out an uncertain laugh, but I knew I was in for trouble.

"Whisper? Why did you bite him?" Asher asked confused.

"It's not what you think! I thought he was a kidnapper. See; obviously, I did the right thing," I stated.

"What do you mean you didn't bite hard! Look, Asher! Do you see my hand? I still have her teeth marks imprinted in it. She is such a liar!" Jaser yanked Asher and forced him to look at his hand.

"I told you, I thought you were a kidnapper!" I yelled once more.

In all seriousness, Jaser quieted down and dropped Asher's hand. "Speaking of kidnapper, it looks like we have company. Not the friendly kind either."

I glanced around as fast as I could, but it was too dark to see anyone. "Asher, can you give us some light?"

Hesitant, he took a step closer to me and formed to balls of fire in his hands. I could see his legs trembling in the small glow of light he had created. Four tall men in suits and sunglasses had surrounded us and stood still. Recklessly Jaser wrapped himself in a veil of electricity and charged towards the tallest man. Barely moving his arm the man, punched Jaser to the ground knocking him unconsciousness.

"That's not good. Any ideas?" I asked, beginning to tremble as well.

Asher shook his head from side to side.

I almost missed the movement of the man on the left because as soon as we through our eyes his way, he tossed some sort of gas grenade on the floor in front of us. "Asher! Put your flames out, hurry!" I screamed.

He did as I said, but soon enough he fell to the ground. The gas from the grenade was spreading with such speed it was getting hard to breath. I had no choice but to collapse as well, losing consciousness with the four looming men engraved in my mind.

Chapter 10

A Camaraderie

As consciousness fought its way back, I felt a cold, bumpy floor below me. My head pounded as if a stampede of elephants had trampled it, and my neck was sore from laying in my current position. I opened my eyes and saw nothing but darkness and a slight rim of light shining behind me, so I could only assume that I was wearing a mask of some kind. It wasn't long before I realized a chain was coiled around my body, tightly trapping my hands to my sides and restricting any movement. Based on the bone-shaking, jolting movement below me, there was no doubt I was in some mode of transportation. The only limbs on my trembling figure that I could move were my legs. Focusing all my mental and physical power on the muscles in my legs, I rose to a wobbling stance.

Oh, great. Where in the world am I now? I can't see anything. It's freezing in here. I hear a loud humming noise, and it smells like sweat. What happened? My whole body hurts. I remember seeing these weird tall men but I don't know what happened after that. Great job, Whisper, you failed once again. Oh, thanks subconscious me. That totally makes me feel a whole lot better. Am I seriously talking to myself right now? Maybe those guys gassed a little more than I thought.

Out of nowhere, it felt like I tilted 180 degrees, and I couldn't stop myself from being thrown against the side wall. The cold, rusty chain dug into my skin, pinching and scraping even more as I rolled on the floor. "Ow!" I yowled, trying to maneuver myself into a position where the chain wasn't pinching my skin.

With the worst timing ever, a large, unknown object crashed into me, knocking me back onto the cold floor. "Ugh," it moaned.

Not again. Why does everyone plow into me? Wait, I know that voice. I could pinpoint that pathetic, ungrateful moan anywhere. I was hoping that he wouldn't be the first person I would run into. Honestly, I don't feel like being murdered by him yet. Why is he here, though? I thought he was left in the town.

"Jaser?" I blindly called out, trying to confirm it was him. "Is that you?"

The silence creeped me out, but eventually, I heard another moan slowly fade into an angry growl. "What the heck? Where am I? Get these stupid chains off me!"

I let out a sigh of relief, not only for the fact he was safe but for the sheer joy I felt knowing he was chained up and had the chance to calm down a bit.

He hesitated for a moment and then jumped to his feet with a loud thud. "Wait a second. Whisper! I'm pretty sure that was your half-witted voice!"

"Whisper? Jaser? My dudes, we ended up together again." Asher shouted.

I couldn't help but smile. "You guys! I'm so glad you are safe! Sorry about this, I had no idea that we were being followed." Even being in their presence made me feel a whole lot better. "Alright! Let's get these chains off."

"How?" Asher asked.

"Well, if I can freeze the piece behind me, then you can smash it with some sort of fire kick," I responded confidently, maybe a little cocky.

"So, what am I supposed to do?" Jaser rudely interrupted.

Almost instinctively, I answered, "Nothing really. I mean, lightning and electricity don't really help us in our situation. Asher, you ready?"

Moving what fingers I could, I managed to tap the chain around me just long enough to send a powerful burst of ice straight through it, freezing it solid.

"Ok. I'll try not to kick you accidentally, Whisper. Sorry if I do," Asher said cautiously.

All I could hear was Asher quickly standing up, and then I felt a quick burning sensation against my skin as the chain shattered and fell to the floor. As I took off my blindfold, I noticed that Asher and Jaser were both covered in scratches and bruises from the fight from earlier.

The section we were in was completely empty, but the surroundings were familiar enough for me to realize that we were in the back of a small cargo plane. It all made sense now, the humming, the cold temperature, and even the sweat. The sweat was mostly coming from Jaser, but I counted it.

"Asher, heat up your chain so I can try breaking it," I said quickly. He struggled for a moment, but eventually, he turned the chain into a steaming string of rust. Encasing my hand in ice, I punched the chain and watched it crumble to the floor.

"Alright. Let's try it at the same time for Jaser." As Asher was taking off his blindfold, I couldn't help but wonder if Jaser was sane enough right now to be released. Then again, Jaser has never been the most rational of sorts.

Simultaneously we attacked the chain using our powers then untied his blindfold.

"About time!" he said as he leaned against the wall, accidentally flipping a switch. "What was that?"

I sighed, and my eyes burst open recognizing what he had done. "That… that is definitely not good! Grab on to something, hurry!"

"But there's nothing in here to grab!" Asher said, startled and confused.

Slowly the hatch of the plane began to open, granting permission for the vacuum-like wind to enter. With all our might, we gripped the floor, but it was no use. We were sliding toward the opening, toward the clear blue sky and the ocean below. The only thing I could think to do was to grab Jaser and Asher. The wind brushed against our faces until at last, we couldn't feel the floor below us. I held to their hands as tightly as I could as we fell from thousands of feet in the air. "I'm sorry! Just hang on to me!" I screamed against the wind.

Asher looked terrified, but he was happy to be back with his friends. "I'm scared! We're going to fall into the ocean and die!"

"Why do I have to die with you fools? Wait...this is kind of fun. I should jump out of planes more often," Jaser yelled

"No one's dying! Well, at least I hope not!" I screamed once more.

Jaser shook his head and pointed with his other hand down toward the ocean. "What do you mean no one is dying? Do you not see how fast we are reaching the ocean?"

"At this speed, we will hit it like cement," Asher nervously added.

I pinched my eyes shut, trying to avoid what was to come. *We can't die here! We have to save the Earth! I know she's out there. I know that sound. Before we fell off the plane, it may have been faint, but that was definitely her. I know for a fact I heard Alzora's wingbeats!*

"Alzora!" I shouted as loud as I could in the hope that my voice would reach hers.

Even when times are tough, or when she may hate me, I couldn't help but become dependent on her. Even then, she showed up. No matter what it was, she was there to protect us, because that's what she is, a protector. I could hear her release her majestic roar as she dived toward us a couple hundred feet above the ocean. It took a few seconds, but once my chest collided with scales, I was confident that we were saved. Somehow, I was the only one who landed on her back. I peered over her side only to see Asher and Jaser hanging in each of her claws like helpless kittens held by the scruff of their necks. She soared into the sky for a moment and then paused, struggling to stay airborne.

"You people are too heavy!" she shouted as she desperately flapped her wings in the air.

"Who are you calling heavy?" Jaser yelled, waving a fist toward her.

"Don't drop us please," Asher pleaded, trying to grab onto her arm with both hands.

Alzora spread her wings into a downward glide and argued, "I can't carry you all."

"Undoubtedly, you frozen eel! I can never comprehend your unbelievable weakness." The familiar smug voice of Zephyr followed behind.

Alzora snapped and turned around just to pick another fight. "What did you call me? You tiny sparkler! Just come and help me already."

"I guess I can take my brat off your hands. Quite literally…" Zephyr shrugged as he glided down next to Alzora tossing Asher onto his back.

"Come on guys, don't fight," Ugi said following behind Zephyr. "Jaser, are you alright?"

"Eh! Chicken, there you are! Why did you run off?" Jaser replied, trying to sound casual.

"I'm truly sorry, but we are back now so don't worry, ok?" Ugi replied shyly.

Quickly leveling herself out, Alzora slapped me with her ear and growled. "What in the world were you thinking back there? You're lucky there weren't any casualties! Oh, and why were you on a plane? Wait…no. Let's rephrase that, why were you falling from a plane? You useless human."

"I'm sorry. I know I messed up, so I'm sorry! I won't let that guy take control of my mind ever again. I refuse. Please forgive me Alzora! All of you. I'm sorry." I apologized. "As for why we were falling…well, we kind of got kidnapped, and then Jaser leaned on the switch that opened the hatch to the plane, which leads us to now."

"Oh, I see, so that's your excuse this time. I guess I can forgive you…wait, what? Go back. What do you mean mind controlled? How the heck were you kidnapped? When could you have possibly been captured? We weren't gone for that long!" She yelled, frustrated and confused.

"Rolland, the guy on the island. He said yeet a lot, which really should have been the first warning sign. Anyway, he drugged the guys over there and then went after me. I was kind of exploring the building at the time…oops. He used this weird device to control me, and that was the last I remembered until I met you guys," I tried to explain.

"Well, great. Now I can't yell at you like I was totally planning to do. It was only partially your fault. Mind controlling? How is that even possible? Whatever, we can't worry about that right now. Explain the kidnapping ordeal!" she ordered, more confused than before.

"I don't know how to explain it! I was just walking along, talking with the others, and these tall guys in suits knocked me out with a gas grenade." I answered.

Jaser stepped in. "Same…I should have killed them all, but they caught me off guard."

"They really had the upper hand on us," Asher added.

Ugi looked back with a worried face. "Are you sure you are alright, Jaser?"

"Chicken, there's no reason why I wouldn't be," Jaser answered, happy to be back.

"How foolish you humans are," Zephyr stated, superior and smug as always.

"Seriously, we can't leave you alone for a whole day without you causing any trouble! I wonder who those humans were." Alzora said.

Ugi flew closer toward me and politely asked, "Whisper, do you happen to know where we are going next?"

"As a matter of fact, I do! I guess somebody caught what looks to be a dragon on camera, but no one is sure what it really was. I looked a bit more into it, and I guess it was a large, feathered, four-legged animal. I think it might be that feather dragon Zephyr mentioned earlier, so why not check it out, right?" I said confidently, ignoring Zephyr's and Alzora's negative comments from before.

Alzora rolled her eyes as if she thought it was really a stupid idea. "So what if it's a dragon? How is that going to help us take down the O.S.I? Come on! I expected more from you…"

I flailed my arms up in the air and argued with her. "What? Ok, ok. Think about it this way. I mean, this dragon must have been living fine without your hidden dragon village's help, so maybe he knows how to defend himself against that organization."

"Besides biting their heads off?" Zephyr interrupted.

"Shh!" I shushed him. "No, I mean maybe he knows enough about them to avoid them. He might even know where their main headquarters is, so why not try it? Right?"

Unsure of himself, Ugi asked his question. "But, is the O.S.I really the cause of all these unnatural phenomena?"

"Indeed. It is troubling to think that a single group of measly humans can deplete the oceans, erupt volcanos, and initiate earthquakes," Zephyr added.

He does have a point, but what else could be causing it? After all, they do have weapons that suck out a dragon's power and use against others.

"Whatever. Where is the feathered dragon?" Alzora asked.

"Oh yeah…um…I know it was in a mountain area. Cam? Caman? Caremon? Oh! Oh! Cameroon!" I was lucky to remember the name; it had completely slipped my mind.

"Where the heck is that?" she asked as she rose into the sky.

"I think in central Africa. How many large green jungles with lush mountains can there be in Africa?" I tried to answer her question to the best of my ability.

"Quite a decent amount, actually," Zephyr said, shooting my reasoning down.

"Oh, well. Just head South. We'll get there eventually!" I yelled, pointing South.

We flew in that direction until the pink and orange skies of dusk greeted us, which took about eight hours.

"Are we almost there?" Asher complained.

"Why don't you try sleeping to pass the time? That's what Jaser is doing." I said kindly, pointing to Jaser who was snoozing on Ugi's shell.

"I tried, but Zephyr's flames keep getting too hot." He added kind of embarrassed.

"Well, I apologize! I cannot help being a dragon, you petty human." Zephyr grunted in frustration.

Alzora slightly turned her direction toward the nearest landmark and dived downward. "My wings hurt. We are going to spend the night here whether you like it or not."

"Fine by me," I mumbled in exhaustion. However, I didn't really feel I had the right to be exhausted since Alzora and the others were the ones who had been flying all day.

The three of them glided toward the landmark, and the closer we got, the more I noticed that there weren't many places to hide. Sand dune mountains covered the land in a way that made the ground look like a muddy sand ocean. I guess Alzora spotted an area before me because she took a sharp turn and headed toward a crater-like area surrounded by hills. "This will work," she said as she curled up in a ball and closed her eyes.

"You're already asleep!" I whispered at her. Soon Zephyr did the same, and Asher crawled up next to him and fell asleep as well. Ugi gently placed Jaser on the cold, hard dirt and curled up around him. I couldn't help but smile. We all were so tired, but at least now we were together. Better yet, we didn't have a problem sleeping so close to each other. Nobody complained about it at all this time. Slowly, I sat next to Alzora and leaned back onto her perfectly coiled tail. The stars above us seemed so different from back home. Even so, I didn't feel like I was that far away. Maybe it was because we had been traveling so much.

Today was pretty weird, I guess. Waking up blindfolded in a small plane was an awful start to the day. Then, I had to go through the embarrassment of apologizing to everyone. Speaking of which, I'm glad that I didn't accidentally wipe out the dragon species. That would have been horrible, but it all turned out ok, so that's good. No one even yelled at me or made fun of me. Well, not any more than they usually do. Maybe they knew my apology was sincere? I don't know. I'm so happy to be back with them. What happened to me? I can't even go a day without them now. Is that just how much our relationship with each other has grown? I can't help but feel that everyone else felt the same way.

"I missed you guys…" I mumbled as I turned to the side, tumbling into my dreams.

It barely felt like we had slept at all when the sun peeked its warm face over a hill, waking us up. Tiny grains of sand flew off the hills, carried in the wind to who knows where. It was unusual for me to be the first one up and awake, but all my friends lay behind me, still sound asleep. I could only assume that it was extra early and that we were in Africa since the sun was just barely rising into the cold, sleepy sky. I watched over my friends, like a tiny guard dog who thinks she's strong enough to take on the world until they awoke. It wasn't long before we were ready to, once again, continue our flight. The land below us switched between mountains, empty safaris, and forests, but eventually, we reached what I thought to be Cameroon.

A lush green forest stretched for miles, and tall mountains rose from the earth. The area itself smelled sweet and was calming. The first thing I noticed was a big waterfall that poured into a muddy brown river. It flowed from the tallest mountain in the forest, and the top of it was unusually flat. Oddly, a rough basketball court and a small house were built there. As we prepared to land, a beam of light shot right pass Alzora and I, almost piercing us. "Woah! What the heck was that?" I yelled.

"Who goes there? Friend or…uh…foe? You're friends, right? Please say friends," a feathered dragon asked as he rose into the sky toward us. His body had regular bright blue and light purple scales, but his chest plates were a bold yellow with dark blue, green, white, and purple feathers poking out of them. His wings were made of complete a mix of bright purple, blue, green, and white feathers as well. His voice had a gentle tone. Not too high, and not too low; it was welcoming.

"I think so?" I replied instinctively.

"Oh good. I'm not one for attacking others. What brings you here my dear friends?" He smiled.

"Vitus?" A teenage boy called from below, purposely enforcing a voice crack when he called. *"Who* are you talking to?"

I couldn't help but yell back at the boy. "Mikau! What on Earth are you doing here?"

"Hey! Whisper! Long time no see! Oh, you know saving the world from high taxes and stuff," he shouted happily.

"Doesn't look like it from up here," I replied and laughed a bit.

"Will you two stop shouting? You're hurting my ears!" Alzora growled.

After landing, I jumped off Alzora and ran over to Mikau. He was about five foot four in height with dirty blonde hair and an extremely short beard. He wore a brown sweatshirt and grey sweatpants.

"I am too! Vitus here is even helping me," he argued playfully.

"Really? Now, how is he doing that?" I asked as if I were winning.

"Not to interrupt you two lovebirds or anything, but how do you know each other?" Alzora said.

Jaser jumped off Ugi and nodded. "I want to know, too."

"Childhood friends. He left a couple of years ago on a mission to save the world from high taxes, but from what I see, it doesn't look like he's gotten that far." I answered.

"Whoa, whoa, whoa…how did you meet Vitus? How long have you known him? How in the world did you get caught in this dragon mess?" I asked.

He shrugged and gave a lame answer. "I was traveling last year and saw him hiding in the city. He liked basketball, so we just started hanging out."

"But…but he's a dragon. How do dragon's even play basketball?" I asked, confused.

"Um…not sure, but he's really good at it," he said.

I sighed, there was no way I was going to understand that logic. "Oh, yeah. Vitus, do you know anything about the O.S.I?"

"Oh, that group? Well, I know their base is like an hour south of here. Stay away from them. They are like pure evil. Lately, they have been kidnapping dragons and stealing their natural power. I have been keeping an eye on them from here, but there isn't much I can do. Instead, I'm trying to help out with your tax problem." Vitus said.

"Would you like to come and help us invade their base? Mikau, I guess you're invited, too," I asked, excited that we might finally have some back up on our missions.

This will be awesome! If we can get some backup, then there's no way that group can take us down.

"No, thank you," he politely declined.

Shocked, I couldn't help but ask why. "Wait, what? But the Earth is dying. Don't you want to help save it? Why not help us?"

"I don't like violence, really. I'm sorry," Vitus apologized.

"Well, there you have it. I guess we stay on our current mission," Mikau jumped in. "Hey, anyone up for a game of basketball before you go?"

Alzora's eyes fired up with determination. "I don't understand how most of your human games work, but the ball just needs to go in the basket, right? You're going down!"

"Dragons against humans?" Asher questioned, worried.

"This is going to be awesome!" Jaser said as he made some practice shots.

"I suck at this game," I mumbled to myself.

The only good players on our team were Mikau and Jaser. Occasionally they would pass the ball to Asher and me, and I would make a couple of shots. The atmosphere was tense as the score evened up, but it felt like this was a good way to relieve all the stress we had. Every time the ball flew toward Ugi he ducked, threw his talons over his head, and accidentally knocked the ball out of bounds with his tail, giving us a free shot. Alzora and Zephyr simultaneously yelled at him when he did that while Vitus just laughed in the background, secretly feeling bad for Ugi.

The main rule of the game was no flying, and with such a small court, the dragons couldn't help but trip on each other's tails. I personally favored the rule of not having to dribble, because I was terrible at that. Every minute or so, both Mikau and Asher would have to step down to tie their shoes. I didn't understand how boy's shoes could come untied so quickly. Everyone there looked like they were having fun and enjoying themselves, and that made me overjoyed.

We took the game up to about thirty points eventually, and we decided to cut it off at thirty-two. It was a pretty even match most of the way, but at last, we had a winner. The humans! I felt a little embarrassed because, throughout the game, Zephyr would accidentally set the ball on fire and Alzora would have to put it out quickly. Somehow, the ball managed to survive the whole game, but I had no idea how. Mikau and I high fived and jokingly bragged about our win to Alzora and Zephyr, which made them mad.

"I guess we should probably go now, though…and save the world," I said, sad because I didn't want to leave.

"Ha, ha. Yeah, that's probably best. I guess I should stay up here and keep an eye on the government so I can find a way to save the world from high taxes," he answered equally disappointed.

As we mounted Alzora and the others and took off, I turned and waved goodbye to Vitus and Mikau. "Goodbye! Thanks for all the fun. Good luck on your mission."

They both waved back at us and shouted, "You, too! Bye!"

It was strange. As we left, I couldn't help but watch as Vitus peered at the grass around the court and spread his wings. Slowly, flowers of all colors sprung through the soil and waved in the wind. Vitus turned once more and locked eyes with me. I couldn't help but wonder why his eyes were so sad. He was clearly smiling and waving goodbye, but his eyes told a completely different story. Was there something I missed or was it just because he hadn't seen his own kind in such a long time? Whatever it was, it gave me an uneasy feeling.

As we grew nearer and nearer to our destination, I could see a previously dormant volcano fuming, and the ground lightly shaking. Dark clouds loomed over the sky and refused to leave. Lightning aimlessly struck around us, and thunder barreled through the skies. We didn't have much time left. If we were going to save the world, we would need to do it now.

Chapter 11

Breached

After a couple of minutes of flying in the direction Mikau and Vitus had pointed out, we reached a distance close enough to spot a sizable building. The building looked out of place in every possible way. To start, it was a pure white half-hexagonal shaped building with no windows, and the only visible doorways were within a triangularly shaped archway on each side. There wasn't a single sign describing what it was, and it was built in the middle of nowhere. The landscape around it was flat with few grass patches, and the oozing volcano was about two miles away. If that building wasn't "suspicious" then I don't know what was. The building itself was utterly silent. Not a sign of life dared be near it. Carefully, we landed a safe distance away in a rock covered area to plan out our attack.

"Question," Asher said. "What are we doing here?"

I almost facepalmed, almost. "Ok. These are the bad guys, right? Therefore, we must stop them, and see if we can get rid of any information they have on dragons. Then, maybe the Earth will live. Just maybe. I don't know. We'll see."

"No way. Is it? Is it…" Jaser started excitedly.

"Yes, Jaser. It's time to…" I sighed, glancing over at the guards heading to the back of the fortress.

Jaser instinctively opened his hands, accidentally spurting lightning bolts everywhere and shouted. "Yes! It's time to bash some heads!"

"Shh, you moron! We don't want to get caught. Well, not yet anyway." Alzora stepped in putting a talon to his lips.

"Please don't kill anyone, Jaser," Asher said, worried.

"Agreed. Jaser, I repeat, don't kill anyone. I'm not sure if that phrase is in your vocabulary, but don't," I said, giving him a severe look.

Jaser rolled his eyes annoyed. "Whatever, I can try, but no promises."

Quickly, noticing guard step out of the white building and look around, Zephyr pushed our heads down. "Quiet," he whispered, keeping an ear out to see if the man made any noise other than a grunt. Once the guard walked back into the building, we continued our conversation.

"Do we have a plan?" Ugi asked quietly.

"I think that's what we are trying to make here, Ugi. Though it's not my fault we aren't making any progress," Alzora said, annoyed.

"Why do you always expect me to make the plan?" I argued with her.

"Um," Asher tried to add.

"Because you tend to be a know it all!" she snapped back.

"Um...hey..." Asher attempted to speak once more.

"I do not!" I yelled, quiet enough not to be heard by the people in the building.

"I have an idea, guys..." Asher said still trying to gain our attention.

"I wouldn't have come if I knew you didn't have a plan!" Alzora fumed.

"Um..." Asher tried to say before being interrupted by Zephyr, who was beginning to feel sorry for the poor boy.

"Listen up you incompetent worms! Try listening to your comrades before arguing about a subject you may already have an answer to," he growled, nudging Asher forward with his tail.

Both Alzora and my eyes locked into an intense stare. "What?" we both yelled simultaneously.

Asher fiddled inside his bag for a second and then pulled out a small drive. I recognized it as his "useless item" that he bought from the store. "I may be able to help with deleting their known information about dragons, nationally."

"How?" Jaser asked intrigued.

"Asher...don't tell me..." I asked, realizing what he did for a living.

He smiled, embarrassed and nodded. "Yep…I'm a hacker. Actually, I downloaded the most recent dangerous computer virus onto this drive when I was in Spain hanging with a friend. I was planning on using it when I got home, but it seems we may need it now."

I was at a loss for words, but Jaser was just as impressed with this as he was about being able to injure people. "I should have guessed it. I knew off the bat you were a total geek, but I didn't expect you to have the sinister mind as well."

"Hey! It's not like that. I only fearsomely hack the people who hacked me first or people who were jerks to me. It's not like I do it to random people," he said, still as innocent as ever.

"Lame!" Jaser mocked.

"Ok, ok, I get the point. That's pretty cool though. I kind of wish I could hack," I added, inspired by Asher's now known skill.

"What's hacking?" Ugi curiously asked.

"A human thing," Alzora said confidently as if she knew everything about it.

"It's not just a human thing; it's a complicated human thing. Asher, you explain. I don't feel like doing it," Jaser answered, not really understanding what it was either.

"Well in simple terms, it means that I can gain access to any computer in the world and mess with their personal information. It really comes in handy when I need to log in to implement a virus and possibly destroy the system," Asher enlightened us.

Zephyr glanced at the entrance and then back at us. "Now that you have settled that matter, how shall we go about invading the targeted building? I personally want some revenge for launching missiles at my village. It is true that everyone managed to survive, but the fact that the O.S.I. intended to murder us all is infuriating."

"You know, we could just storm in there," I suggested, running out of ideas.

"It's official, that is literally the worst idea you have had. See, I told you she was crazy," Alzora teased.

"Ok, I'll admit it. That idea was pretty bad." I scratched my head as if it would pull up ideas from deep within.

"My turn. Sorry if this is a bad idea. What if we acted like we were a part of their group? Like new recruits or something," Ugi blurted.

"Did you forget that we are dragons? We can't just waltz in there. They would try to kill us," Alzora hissed, shooting the idea down.

"Hold up. I think Ugi's onto something! We could act like new recruits and just say that you're our prisoners." I smiled in accomplishment.

"What an unfeasible idea," Zephyr remarked. "I refuse to be a human's prisoner, even if it is an undercover scheme."

Asher gently patted his tail and smiled. "Oh, come on, Zephyr. It's only until we arrive inside. After all, it is our only option."

Jaser was going to burst from excitement. "Alright, can we go already?"

"Hold on. We need to cover some rules. One, avoid any type of weapon they may have, even if it looks like a toy. Two, if we happen to get separated, we fight our way back after ensuring the files are destroyed. Three, we need to find whatever is causing Earth's annihilation. Ok, I'm done now; we can go." Quickly, I mounted Alzora's back and gave the building a determined glare.

We landed behind the building as stealthily as possible and carefully we jumped onto the rumbling dirt without making a peep. As we slowly approached one of the large triangular entrances, with the dragons following close behind, we made contact with what looked to be a camera. For some odd reason, the door opened by itself and practically invited us in. It was a pretty great plan until Alzora started improvising. "You idiotic human! How dare you capture us?"

This time, I really did facepalm, and I wasn't too shocked that her tone and attitude toward me now was like our normal relationship. The inside of the building was just as clean and white as the outside, and surprisingly, there weren't many people around. The strange thing was that the people who were stationed inside just nodded and walked away. Our plan was actually working.

Something's not right. Not a single person is questioning us. It's as if this is normal for them. This place is like a maze. How are we supposed to find a room with Alzora and them following us the whole time? I guess for right now, I just have to remain silent and act like I know what I'm doing, which I really don't.

As we passed from one hall to the other, I noticed that the rooms on the sides each contained laboratory equipment. Most of the rooms consisted of a desk, a microscope, and frighteningly sharp tools. The farther into the building we went, the more confusing the halls became.

"Would you follow me please?" I was startled by the large man who stepped beside me.

"Oh...sure...may I ask why?" I stuttered.

"You're the new recruits in charge of this month's dragon shipment, correct?" he asked as he guided me down an even longer hall.

I can't believe our stupid plan is working.

"Yes...it is amazing how quickly word gets around about new recruits." Nervous, I continued with my chain of lies.

"We try to have the best communication possible here in case a sneaky, maniacal dragon tries to invade." The man seemed to be enjoying the conversation.

What is up with this guy? I mean, that's exactly what we are doing.

"I see. That is indeed efficient." I nodded, trying to keep my legs from trembling.

"Did you hear about our most recent successful mission?" He gave a concerned and confused glance at my trembling legs but continued walking.

"No, I haven't. What happened?" Part of me knew what he was going to say next, but no matter what it was, I had to focus on maintaining my self-control.

"Executive Rolland easily tricked a group of foolish teenagers into launching a missile at the dragon's territory." I could feel the heat fuming from Zephyr's nostrils and the growl slipping from Alzora's mouth as the man continued his enjoyable conversation. "I wonder what some pesky kids were doing on that island, to begin with. Rolland attempted to exterminate them since they knew about the dragons, but he failed. Our orders are to keep a look out for them."

"Thank you for the update," I said with fake gratitude.

Eventually, we stopped in front of a straight hallway with bright lights hanging from the ceiling. I could smell the undistinguishable aroma of blood coming from the hallway, and it made me want to vomit.

Was this where he was sending us? The dragon killing room? Why? Why do I smell this? I can't stand it! I don't want to go in there!

"Anyhow, this is where we shall be parting. Straight down that hall is the lab, so just take the subjects down there. Don't forget to keep an eye out for those teens. The troublesome one was a girl with a pair of goggles on her head and hair with a few braids. The other one was a stupid looking fellow with white hair, and the last one had gla…" He stated as he slowly turned, recognizing our faces.

Well, that didn't take long. Besides, there's no way I want to go down that hallway right now. Not until I can get that odor out of my nostrils. This guy definitely isn't the sharpest knife in the drawer. I mean he had a full description of us and everything, and he still didn't put it together until now.

"Y-you are… You are those kids. Security! All units to section four! We've been breached. I repeat we have been breached! Bring every weapon possible." He screamed as he ran down the aisle with his puffy cheeks bouncing along the way.

On his way down, he slammed a silver button on the wall, setting off an alarm that I assumed was for us. We had no choice but to run. We were running out of time, and we needed to find that main system room quickly. My heart throbbed as we ran through the siren-filled building, trying to dodge enemies at every corner. Amid all the chaos, I lost track of where Asher had disappeared to. He wasn't with us anymore. "Guys! Where's Asher?"

"I don't know. Keep running! Those are very scary humans!" Ugi shouted toward me from behind.

Zephyr sped up and took a quick glance back. "He probably recognized the main system room as we were fleeing. I am certain he is fine. He knows his job."

We turned from one corner to the next until we reached a blockade of guards in long lab coats, forcing us to come to a halt. It wasn't long before hundreds of them had surrounded us, each carrying an odd-looking weapon. "We are going to die!" Ugi gasped as he braked with his back legs.

"M-maybe?" I stammered.

Alzora slammed her tail against the floor and hissed at the guards. "I'm done running! I don't get why we even ran in the first place. You foolish humans! How dare you think that you can even begin to come close to the power of an ice dragon? I will destroy all of you!"

"Hey! Frozen fillet, leave me a substantial amount! I would enjoy thrashing a couple of humans. I haven't done something this exciting in ages." Zephyr immediately lifted his flaming tail and knocked out a dozen people with one swing.

"No fair, you had a head start!" Alzora whined. "Whisper," she said in all seriousness. "You said these weapons are made from the absorbed natural power of dragons, right? Meaning, they could have anything from hypnotism, to wind, poison or even death itself. This could get dangerous, so I want you to go."

"No! I want to help you. What if something happens? Since when do I ever do what you say?"

"Hey, I want to bash some heads in, too!" Jaser exclaimed.

"Shut up, you stupid humans! I said go, so go!" Alzora growled.

"Alzora! I don't want to leave you again. Please," I pleaded.

"Ugi! Take them and go! Oh, and keep this in mind: if you die, I am seriously going to kill you!" For the first time, Alzora looked truly worried, and I didn't understand why. Couldn't she take on a couple of humans, or was she worried about taking them on and not killing them? Even from my distance, I could tell that she was serious. Her usual round pupils reduced to tiny slivers, and the guards had stolen all her attention.

Nervous, Ugi took a running start and grabbed both Jaser and I in his talons as he lifted into the air, flying over the crowd of guards. The building halls were just wide enough for him to let out his full wingspan. If it were Alzora or Zephyr, there would be no chance of flying out.

"No!" I screamed and struggled. "Let me go! I need to help them!"

"Whisper, please. I'm sorry. I know you want to help, but honestly, how much help could you be? There are hundreds of those people with deadly weapons, and if you two were involved, Alzora and Zephyr wouldn't be able to go all out. Instead, they would have to keep an eye on you two. Please! Trust me on this!" Ugi apologized as he hesitantly flew down the hall we came from. The hall that smelt of blood. The hall that painfully tore my heart into pieces.

We soon reached a large open room with massive, liquid-filled tubes built into the wall. They fizzed as if they were pumping into a generator, but with a closer look, I was horrified to see what was inside of the tubes. Each tube held a dead dragon glowing with a yellow light, and I couldn't bear to keep my eyes on it for more than a second. It made me sick. Some of the tubes were stained with blood. It was as if they injured the poor dragon and left him in there to drown. Others had scratch marks on the side, and some of the dragon's tails had been cut off and were floating in the liquid. Tears formed in Ugi's eyes and trickled down his face as he looked from one dragon to another. From behind us, a skinny blond woman crept up and rested her spiraled gun like device on her shoulder, and she blew a puff of smoke from her cigarette.

"Like what you see? Miraculous, ain't it? It never gets old; that is, watching the magic and life get sucked outta you monsters. Serves you right."

"How could you do this?" I bellowed at her.

"It's…It's not magic. It's just how our body functions. Why don't you leave us alone? I know you humans aren't all bad. Why? Why are you hurting us like this?" Ugi cried.

"This is totally messed up, you hag." Jaser spat at her.

"What did you just call me, you incompetent child? Here I am, being generous and showing you some of the wonderful things in life, and you call me a hag! You filthy rat!" She answered astonished.

"Shut up," Jaser said casually giving her his evil "serious" eyes.

"You little! I'll make you regret the day you were born!" With the flip of a switch on her gun, she pointed it at us and maniacally laughed.

My body felt heavy as something pulled it to the ground below me. I couldn't stand up, nor move any part of my body. The pressure felt like it was going to break my spine in two. The only way to prevent my agonized screams was to grit my teeth together and chomp down hard. No matter the pain, I refused to lose my consciousness. To my right, Jaser was having the same trouble. He stayed upright longer than I did, but eventually, he succumbed to the gravitational force as well.

I couldn't believe what he managed to say, but I indeed heard him right. "Ugi, do something!" Jaser said Ugi's name for the first time since they had met each other. Was Jaser really that desperate, or did he want Ugi to learn to fight when he needed to?

"Oh, shut up, brat," the woman snarled as she increased the force on the device.

Jaser couldn't help but let out a gasp for air. The force was becoming too much. It had reached the point of crushing our lungs.

It hurts! I don't know how much longer I can keep this up. I can't move at all, and it feels like the force is crushing the life out of me. It's getting harder to breathe. What can I do, though? Ugi, I know that you are in just as much pain as we are, but you are our only hope. I mean, you are a dragon after all.

Ugi's pupils were reduced to a barely noticeable sliver as he fumed through his nose and picked up one talon. Using all his strength, he pulled himself to a standing position and directed a death glare at the lady forcing us to the ground. Electricity radiated from his body and fused with the small amount coming from Jaser.

He was unrecognizable. Where was the kind, paranoid, nervous dragon we all new? All I could see in front of me was an uncontrollable, infuriated dragon who would lash out at any moment. Ugi had snapped to a point beyond words and imagination. He slowly smiled, cracked his wrists and aimed a bolt of electricity at the middle-aged woman, annihilating the gravity device.

Immediately, I felt relief, and I rose to a staggered stance, my back still sore from all the pressure. Jaser stood just as quickly and shot me a glance. "Whisper, go find the geek. We got it covered here."

"I see. So this is how you want to play?" The woman grinned as she brought out a shield and another gun.

Ugi stared at me with is neon green eyes before I left. He looked as if he were a wild animal getting ready to mutilate his prey. It was enough to make me slightly afraid, but I didn't want to be.

Hesitantly, I turned toward an exit in the room and started running. I knew I could leave that woman in their hands. I knew once I watched their power fuse. It was an act of complete trust. There was no way they could lose.

I have to find Asher! I need to make sure the files are destroyed. Where is he, though? He must be somewhere near here since he didn't disappear too long after we reached the second corner. Oh my gosh! This place is like a maze! I'm not going to find anything, correction anyone, at this pace. I must, at the very least, be able to do this! Ugi, Alzora, Zephyr, and even Jaser are all fighting out there to make sure we accomplish our goal.

I wonder what those large test tubes in that room with the crazy lady were for, though. I don't know what they could have been pumping to, but I'm pretty sure it's not good. There is definitely the possibility that those tubes are behind all of these phenomena, but I don't know. Either way, with the combined forces of Jaser and Ugi, they are bound to get destroyed, even if by accident. I mean, usually Ugi is harmless, but he had that look in his eyes that evoked pure horror. If he and Jaser fight together side by side, who knows what they can do. They both had a frightening lust for blood. It gives me the shivers just thinking about it. I have to trust them, though. No matter how dimwitted those two guys may seem, I need to put all my faith in them. Asher, on the other hand, where is he?

My enthusiastic, determined run eventually faded into a pathetic, out of breath walk as I went by each room. The ground was beginning to tremble below me, and now cracks began to form on the ceilings and walls. They were going to fall at any moment. My only guess to the cause was the earthquakes, dying world, and all that fun stuff.

As the bitter smell of something burning rose to my nose, I couldn't help but get the sinking feeling that something had gone horribly wrong. I couldn't see much in front of me except for the broken, hanging, flickering lights. I could smell something burning, yet I did not see any smoke. Cautiously, I crept through each hall, expecting some bad guy to pop out of the shadows like in those cliché stories, but I did not see a soul. I assumed that they were all fighting against the others, but it was odd not to see anyone.

It wasn't long before I began to feel light-headed, and it was becoming difficult to breathe. However, I continued to move forward. With what little energy I had left, I squinted at the closed door in front of me and noticed a warm glow underneath. Idiotically, I opened the door, welcoming a face full of flames. From what I could see, the room was ginormous. Filing cabinets lined the walls and a large computer and control panel was in the center. Amidst the flames, a figure waved his hands in the air and frantically stomped on the fire. I coughed a couple of times which I guess gave away my position.

The figure turned and ran his hands through his hair terrified. "Whisper, I accidentally set the place on fire."

"Asher! There you are! I have literally been scrambling through this place for the past half hour," I managed to spurt out. "Did you implement the virus, though?"

"I hacked the systems but…" he mumbled, scratching his arms in the flames.

"Wait, how did you set the place on fire? Was someone attacking you or something? Please tell me you have a legit reason," I asked, desperate for an answer.

He shook his head and glanced down. "Well, you see…I hacked the system, which by the way was really complicated. You wouldn't believe how many networks they were connected to across the world. I had some time to spare, so I looked for anything that might give us a clue on how they are causing these phenomena. Out of the millions of files on the mainframe, only one contained what we were looking for. There wasn't much in it, but it mentioned something about having connections with a new deadly weapon that they would use to destroy all dragon kind. Dude, there was literally no detail on what the weapon is or how it works, but from what I do know, that weapon is the source of our dying planet."

"Really? That's great! All we need to do now is find that weapon and destroy it, right? Can't be too difficult? Hold up, how did the fire start? You didn't answer my question," I asked, still curious as to what had happened.

"I didn't mean to. I just was so excited when I accomplished my mission, that I accidentally, subconsciously sparked the control panel. It caught on fire and then spread to the computer, which kind of exploded. Now here we are surrounded by flames, but, hey, I got the job done, right?"

"But did you really get the job done?" spoke a familiar voice in the distance. I couldn't pinpoint exactly how I knew the voice, but something about it sounded familiar.

Asher hopped backward and bolted next to me, jumping through the flames as he ran. "What do you mean by that?"

A loud sucking noise filled my ears as I watched the flames deplete one by one, each vacuumed into a small handheld device. My vision almost immediately improved, but a glimpse of a silver strand of hair made me wish it hadn't. There hiding in the shadows was Ciara, with her purple-tipped, silver hair flowing behind her.

She bore the smile of a demon and wore a tight-fitting suit, far superior to any of the other lackeys we had come across. "Oh, Whisper. What have you gotten yourself into? Over the years, I really did come to trust you. Now, yes now...now you have allied yourself with these evil beasts. Too bad, though, I was hoping I wouldn't have to get my hands dirty. I have been keeping an eye on you since the very beginning. I knew you and your so-called friends would come for us eventually, but I wasn't expecting you to do so this soon. Oh well, now that you have practically ruined all my plans, I think it is finally time to kill you pests.

Isn't that right, Beckett?"

Chapter 12

The True Destroyer

I couldn't believe my ears nor my eyes. Was this girl really the kind and caring Ciara I grew up with? The same Ciara who supported me through all my troubles? The same optimistic Ciara who wouldn't hurt a fly? There beside her stood Beckett with a shy, guilty expression on his face.

"You aren't Ciara!" I screamed. "She would never, never, do something like this!" I spoke in the hope that my words could become the truth, but I knew that it wasn't the case.

"Oh, silly girl, don't lie to yourself. You know it's me!" She shouted back with a smug smile. It was written all over her, by her stance, voice, hair, even a part of her attitude. Everything about her was my best friend, and there was no way I could deny the truth for much longer. The real question was why. Why was she doing this?

Has my whole life really been a lie? This isn't real. I must be dreaming or something, right? What is wrong with her? I have known her for ten years. There's no way that she was just a spy this whole time. How could I not have noticed something like this? Why? Why is this happening? What is up with Beckett, too? I mean, I don't know him very well, but he didn't look like he had an ounce of evil in him when we first met. What is he doing here?

176

"Please stop this. It isn't like you, Ciara," I desperately cried out. "Why are you and Beckett doing this?"

"Why? What kind of question is that? To annihilate the dragon race, of course. Why else would I do this? Those dragons think they can do whatever they please without consequence, but it's time they learn who the real rulers of this planet are," she shouted in frustration.

"What are you talking about? Why do humans have to be the only rulers? We only have one Earth. Why can't we just share it with them? Not only the dragons but every creature. Why can't we all live together, in peace?" I couldn't help but shake my head in confusion.

"Because! Those monsters are selfish and dangerous, not to mention they feel that we are inferior to them!"

"But that isn't the whole truth! Sure, Alzora and Zephyr are extremely selfish at times and rude, and they tend to have a superior attitude, but that's just because they are dragons and that's what dragons do! Yeah, they are strong, and sometimes they are so terrifying that I think they want to murder me—" I said honestly before being interrupted.

"Ha! You admitted it. They are practically demons." Ciara pointed at me and laughed.

"I wasn't finished. They may be scary and rude, but they are also kind and caring. I can't even count how many times they have saved us and forgiven us for what stupid things we did. And, how dare you call them dangerous when you are the one singling them out and torturing them to death! From what I see, you are the dangerous one here," I muttered.

"I'm not arguing with you. If you refuse to understand the potential of the destructive creatures, then I am finished with you! I thought I might be able to make you change sides, but I see that that is no longer a possibility."

"Listen! Those dragons that are fighting out there, they are my friends. And guess what? That human fighting out there, and even this guy beside me, they are my friends, too. I don't care whether they're human or dragon, they are my friends, and I refuse to let you break my bond with them!" I yelled at her.

"If that's the way you want it, then die!" She turned and slowly walked through the doors behind her. "Beckett, kill them, torture them, make them die in the most painful way possible. I'll leave it up to you."

Beckett silently nodded and pulled a device from his jacket pocket. I could recognize that device anywhere. It was the same white device with a neon glow that Rolland used to control my mind back at the island. He was aiming it at Asher, but I couldn't let that happen, not to him. If he did something, he would never be able to forgive himself. I could sense the laser of light cover my skin as I shoved him out of the way.

I took a deep breath as the negative thoughts poured through my mind. However, this time was different. I felt a little more in control of my thoughts.

No! Go away! I won't let you take over my head again. I don't want to hurt my friends, never again.

My vision flickered for a minute, but then I realized that I could see. I could see, but I couldn't control my body. I knew my body was moving, but I couldn't do anything to stop it. I couldn't even speak. All I knew was that I was walking toward Asher, backing him against a wall. It was then, at that moment, the darkness that had been stalking me took hold of me again. To the right of us, Beckett stood creepily, smiling with a small pistol in his hand. "Kill him."

I knew my body was moving forward as I reached my hands toward his throat, tightly gripping it. I couldn't get the look of his face out my head. His breaths were quick and short, and his eyes were spread open in terror.

Stop! Hands, I command you to stop. Please stop! If this keeps up, I really am going to kill him. He looks so scared. Asher, it's not me. Set me on fire or something. Stop me. Stop me, Asher! I don't want to hurt you.

I could feel tears falling down my cheeks onto his face, but I still couldn't control my body. It was almost like he could read my thoughts because he smiled. Asher put on his big grin like always. He knew I couldn't control it. He understood he was quite possibly going to die, yet he smiled. It was a smile that attempted to say it's ok, a smile that made my heart ache. My head raced from worry as I watched him fall into unconsciousness.

Asher! No! You're not allowed to die, you idiot. Stop!

Convinced that Asher was going to die soon, Beckett pointed the pistol at both of us and took a shot with his eyes closed, as if this was a game. I couldn't really feel the pain, but a shiver raced up and down my spine, and my leg throbbed.

You are going to pay for this. Stop this stupid mind control, or body control, crap this instant. I hope you are ready for the world of pain you're about to be in.

Anger boiled in and out of my body as I managed to yell and pull my hands off Asher. I didn't even bother to look down at my leg. My anger numbed the pain. Beckett backed up, startled, and shot at me clumsily once more, missing his target. This time, it was my turn to snap.

I screamed as I hardened my fist with a coat of ice and punched Beckett in the side. With my non-injured leg, I roundhouse kicked him in the head and shoved him to the ground, quickly knocking him unconscious.

"Asher!" I yelled, running over to him checking his pulse. I fell over in relief to find that he was still alive. My relaxation was short lived as a jolt of pain shot through my blood gushing leg. I could barely breathe through the pain as I grabbed it and rolled on the floor in agony. I held in my screams, but tears formed in my eyes as I bit my lip. I ripped my jacket off and quickly tied it around my leg to stop the blood flow. I had no choice but to sit on the floor for a minute and take a breath. The fire had torched the room around me, and small pieces of the ceiling crashed to the ground.

I have to get him out of here. I can't stand, and this place is falling to the ground. All our fighting must have done a number on the place. I wonder how the others are doing. I hope they are ok. I just need to rest for a minute then, I think I can make a break for it. Maybe if I put up an ice shield barrier, we will be safe for at least a little bit.

Slowly I tightened my finger muscles, and in a pulling motion toward the ground, I created a pile of ice that soon rose into a dome-like shape above us, leaving us a door-like opening. Pebbles of concrete tapped onto the barrier above us. I glanced down at Asher with his broken glasses and frowned. "I'm so sorry."

The guilt that I felt caused me more pain then the wound in my leg.

I may not have been able to prevent all destruction, but at least I was able to save Asher. I don't understand why Ciara and Beckett are so set on murdering the dragons. Beckett kind of seems like a puppet. He hasn't said a word since we met him. Well, besides the command he gave for me to kill Asher. Even behind his evil exterior, I could still see those sad eyes. What is going on? Is Ciara really the one behind this? Why can't she just understand? Dragons and humans can live in harmony. *We may not be at the point where the whole world can find out about them, but we definitely should be able to live together without conflict. They have been doing so for centuries, and it wasn't until recently that this mess started up.*

Why exactly is the Earth dying? And the legend, what's up with that? I mean, the descriptions were accurate, but I still don't understand how we are the ones who are going to destroy the planet. Little by little, I feel like this is adding up, but I need more information. This just isn't enough.

What's that? I glanced into the hall through the broken section of the wall. I could hear a voice mumbling to himself and talons colliding with the shards of broken glass and concrete. I felt weak, almost too weak to speak, but I managed to yell. "Hey! In here!"

He was still a far away, but I knew that I was looking at the unmistakable flames of Zephyr. As he drew nearer, I noticed several new scrapes and bruises on his scales. If he was here, then where was Alzora? Was she alright?

Quickly, he entered the room and blinked at Asher and I. "Am I correct to assume that our mission is complete here?"

"Yes. Asher did a great job of destroying the files. Zephyr can you do me a favor?" I asked.

"Wonderful. A favor?" He raised his eyes and leaned closer to me.

"Take Asher out of here. The building is collapsing, and he still hasn't woken up yet."

"I was planning on it but what about you?"

"Just take him and hurry. I have something I need to take care of first." I glanced at Beckett and back at Zephyr.

Zephyr seemed exhausted. He didn't have the energy to act like his smug, superior self. He managed to nod and gently pick up Asher and set him on his scaly back. "I suggest you move quickly as well. This building was not meant to sustain this much pressure and damage."

"Wait," I said as he turned to leave, "is Alzora ok?"

He hesitated and then turned toward me. "Unfortunately, I do not know. We split up mid-battle, taking half of the enemies with us."

That had me worried, but I knew there was no possible way Alzora would lose. I wasn't entirely sure why I stayed behind, because I really didn't have anything specific to do. Maybe, part of me wanted to save Beckett.

"Ok, you jerk. Let's get out of here. You're lucky that the bullet mostly grazed my leg," I said to his unconscious body. He was tall, but he wasn't that heavy, making it easier on me. The pain in my right leg had decreased quite a bit, and I managed to stand up with my one good leg picking up Beckett in the process. I slung his arm around my back and neck. The room smelled like burnt paper and heat continued to radiate from the ground. I managed to stand on my feet, but it was difficult to walk forward. I limped with each step, but I couldn't afford to give up this early. I dragged both our injured bodies to the edge of the hallway and rested on the wall for a minute. Behind me, the roof of the room collapsed, crushing my ice dome barrier into tiny shards.

"Oh man, that was close," I said aloud.

Zephyr was right. This building really isn't going to last much longer. I just need to get out of here. If I make it outside, I can see if all the earthquakes and phenomena have stopped yet. After all, if this building goes down, I'm sure whatever weapon they are hiding will be destroyed as well. Then again, Ciara is still around here somewhere, unless she already escaped. I hope that she isn't carrying the weapon with her because that would make things a lot worse. Ok, calm down, Whisper; just focus on getting out of here alive for right now.

At this point, there was barely any lighting, and the lights that were on were dangling from the ceiling about to snap. I tried to hurry down the hall, but because I was carrying the weight of both Beckett and myself on an injured leg, I wasn't making much progress. My leg felt like it was going to give out soon, but I had to hang it in there for a little while longer. My whole body ached from my toes to my shoulders, and even my head pounded. Debris covered the aisle making it difficult to move forward. "I can't believe you shot at me. Like, you shot at me with a real gun. Who does that? You people are so messed up."

184

The ground began to shake once more below me, but this time it made the whole building rumble. I fell to the ground, failing to keep my balance.

This isn't good. That weapon must not be destroyed yet. Crap, I can't stand back up. The ground is shaking way too much. What do I do? If I stay here, I'm bound to get squashed by the ceiling, but I can't get up! Actually, it's ok. If Alzora and the others are ok, then I am fine with this fate. They don't need me. I will just drag them down. As long as they are safe, it's ok.

I rolled onto my back and stared at the crackling ceiling above me. "It's not that I'm giving up, I just can't move, that's all. I'm sorry, Beckett. I really wanted to save you and see this through to the end. You know, the funny thing is I really don't want to give up here, and I really don't feel like dying. I mean, seriously, I am even talking to you, and you're unconscious. I really must be going crazy."

"Told you." There it was, the voice I adored, the voice of a friend, the voice of loyalty, the voice of Alzora. She replied in such a calm way, her relief could have been unrecognizable to anyone else.

I turned my head to the side to see Alzora with her head bent down staring at me. "Alzora! You're ok. I'm so glad—"

"Oh, be quiet already. Let's get out of this heap of rubble. Did you happen to see that flame head pass by here?" Quickly yet carefully, she wrapped her tail around me and set me on her back. She put Beckett on her back with less delicacy.

185

"I didn't even hear you coming. Yeah, Zephyr took Asher a little while ago, so they should be out of here by now." I said exhausted, messing with her ears.

"Good. That means we are the last to escape. I saw Ugi and Jaser off a while ago, so let's hurry and catch up." As she rose, the ground continued to grumble below us, and the pieces of the ceiling fell both in front and behind us.

I couldn't control the amount of pain my body was in, but I knew that I would be safe as long we could make it out of here. As Alzora raced through the halls, I could feel the dirt-like powder tap my head, keeping me from dozing off. It didn't help that the powder substance made me want to sneeze. It was hard to believe that this building was the same one we originally came into seemingly so long ago. When we first arrived, everything was clean, orderly, and bright from the lighting, but now everything was a mess. Most of the rooms we passed were pitch black, and the halls were dimly lit, making it difficult to see where we were going. Patches of the ceiling were on the floor, and occasionally we would come across a hole in the roof showing the stormy sky above. Unfortunately, the holes were too small for either of us to crawl through.

Alzora didn't bother to look back, but I knew she was directing her question toward me. "What happened in there? I noticed your leg is bleeding, too. What's up with that?"

I didn't want to answer her question. How was I supposed to tell her that we were saving the man who tried to kill me, the same man who almost forced me to strangle Asher? She didn't even know that Beckett had been a spy this whole time. What was I supposed to say?

Then it hit me. I knew exactly what to say. "Honestly, I don't know what happened. To tell you the truth, I'm not sure what's going on here. My childhood friend, Ciara, claims to be the boss of the operation, and for some reason, she is dead set on killing me, no pun intended. Beckett…he…I mean Ciara says he's a spy, but I refuse to believe that. Maybe it's all an act. Please don't be mad Alzora. He may have been the one to shoot me, but don't hurt him! I don't think we are getting the whole story.

I could have sworn that she was going to stop in her tracks right there, but instead, she continued to run. I knew by her shift in breathing that she was infuriated. "I see. So she's the true culprit. Why in the world are you saving Beckett? He's a traitor! We should leave him right here. Let him die along with this place. That is an odd wound. What did he shoot you with?"

"Ugh. You're not listening to me! It doesn't matter what he shot me with, it grazed me that's all. It was just a small pistol. I'll be fine. I told you we don't have the whole picture, anyway. I don't know why, but I don't think it's his fault." I said, grasping her horns.

"You really are such a moronic, insane girl. How could you let yourself get injured in battle, let alone believe the enemy didn't do it intentionally?"

I glanced down at her roughed-up scales and snickered. "What are you talking about? You got hurt, too, you know. But I really don't think he meant to do it."

"Whatever. Ok, miss smarty pants, how do you figure he's so innocent?"

"I haven't got that far yet," I admitted as I scratched my head.

"I saw that response coming. I can't believe you. Why do you always leave it until the last minute to figure things out? We don't even know how we are going to stop this disaster yet."

"Oh, I almost forgot! When Asher was hacking the system, I guess he found this secret file containing information about some deadly weapon that may be causing the phenomena."

"Well, it looks like you two accomplished something, at least. Where is this so-called weapon?" Alzora asked as she dodged a falling piece of ceiling.

"That's the problem. I think Ciara took it with her when she escaped."

"I take it back. You two are idiots."

"Hey, it's not our fault we never actually saw the weapon. As I said, Asher just read some stuff about it. I wish we knew more, but that's all we got."

"Hm…still doesn't seem like a believable excuse." It was like she was just trying to make me mad at this point.

"What do you want me to say? Hey Alzora, we found some magical destruction weapon and disintegrated it. Sorry, I'm not that perfect."

"I should have expected that. You are a human after all. Then again, not even dragons are perfect beings. After all, we aren't God."

"I guess we can agree on that. Hey, is that the exit?" I pointed excitedly toward the glowing door.

Alzora quickly increased her speed and took a ginormous leap through the door, avoiding the dangerous sections of the triangular archway attempting to collapse onto us. I wasn't sure how, but the surroundings looked worse than they did when we had first arrived. Thunder crackled through the skies, and lightning struck the nearest trees in a rampage. I realized that the reason it was so dark outside wasn't just because of the clouds. Lava was leaking from the volcano, and smoke rose to the sky covering the dark clouds.

Ugi and Jaser were the first to notice us, so we ran over to them to recuperate. They looked a little banged up but nothing too serious. As expected, Ugi had returned to his usual nervous, worried, paranoid self, which was a relief for me. To the left of us, Zephyr and Asher flew downward to our little group. I was happy to see Asher awake and optimistic like always. He smiled and waved at us. When they landed, he hopped off and walked over to me. I wasn't sure what he was going to say, but I was ready to apologize.

"Dude, I had a really weird dream. You were like trying to strangle me, but you were crying as you did it. I'm glad you're ok because it kind of worried me," he said with a huge grin on his face.

His neck was still red and a little swollen, but I decided to play dumb for his sake. It was better for everyone if he just believed it was a dream. "Um…yeah. That does sound really weird."

"You guys should have seen us. We were totally awesome! Once the Chicken and I figured out how to combine our electricity, we fried that hag," Jaser interrupted.

Ugi attempted to shush him, but he failed. "Jaser, no need to go that far!"

Zephyr glanced up toward the hostile sky and mumbled to himself, "It seems every one of us, both human and dragon, has had a rough time on this mission. Surprisingly, we all made it out alive. We must not be destined for death yet."

Maybe that is because we are destined to cause death. At least no one has noticed my leg yet. I really don't want them to make a big deal. The less they know, the better, but I should probably explain the whole Beckett and Ciara scenario.

That's exactly what I did, and, for the most part, all but Asher reacted in the same way that Alzora did. I managed to calm them down in the same way I did with Alzora, but we did end up on agreeing to lay Beckett down on the soil behind us while we came up with a plan.

Before we could do anything, the ground began to violently shake once more, knocking all of us to the ground. Carefully balancing on the rolling earth, we mounted the dragons and rose into the smoke-filled sky to get a better look at the situation. What we found astonished us.

Below, a dragon's paw burst through the soil. Next came his head and the other paw. His scales were the color of ash, and it looked as if darkness itself was beneath each individual scale. His roar bellowed through the sky, almost blowing us away. The most terrifying thing about this dragon was that his paw alone was the size of Alzora's body. There he lay, his body halfway emerged, staring at me with his greedy, gold eyes that seemed to thirst for destruction.

Chapter 13

To Live or Die

"What is that?" I screamed in terror as the humungous dragon emerged from the earth.

Zephyr shook his head, dumbfounded. "For once in my life, I do not have the slightest clue as to what that being is."

I was grateful that we fled to the sky when we did, because below us the ground ripped apart, creating ravines. By some miracle, they kept a distance from Beckett who was still unconscious on the dry crackling dirt.

I couldn't concentrate because of Ugi's vocal terror. "Oh my...oh my...We are all going to die! I mean it this time! That...that thing is going to kill us. Are you sure the legend said that we are going to destroy the world because I'm pretty sure it's the other way around? Sorry, I'm complaining too much. It's more likely that he is going to destroy us, then the planet."

"Jeez, Chicken, calm down. Come on. We can take him no prob!" No matter how cocky Jaser was acting, I could see the alarm in his eyes.

I, on the other hand, was going through another vision. *Perfect timing.* All I could see was destruction, and it wasn't the giant dragon's doing either. The grass was lit with flames all around me, to the point where I couldn't see any of my friends. The soil that wasn't covered in burning grass was covered with a layer of burning ice. The hair on every inch of my body stood from the static and electricity that flowed through the ground. It defied every law of nature that I was taught. The same effect went on for miles, killing everything in sight. I couldn't grasp how I was the only one left, but I was. Behind me, the titanic dragon slept, and above me, Alzora, Ugi, and Zephyr rampaged through the skies, annihilating everything in their path. They were acting like wild animals. I mean, they were wild animals, but it wasn't like them. Their only emotions were anger and hatred toward the planet.

What did it all mean? Was the legend right? Are our combined powers going to destroy everything we know and love? How did this happen? Then, it clicked. One subtle sign made it clear. One single tear, a tear of pain and sorrow fell from one of them onto my skin, and I immediately knew. They were being controlled. By who, I had no idea, but I was certain that they couldn't control a single one of their actions. The question is how, and how do Asher, Jaser, and I factor into the legend, if at all? If the dragons were going to end up doing this, then why would they have needed us?

I pondered on this for a long while as the dragon pulled the last of itself onto the horrid land. As I suspected, Ciara stood on top of the dragon's nose with her arms crossed. She was a mouse compared to him and his enormous body.

Was this the weapon she was talking about? We were such fools to believe that it was an object. What the heck is she doing with a

193

dragon? I thought she hated dragons. I don't understand what's happening!

"Alzora. Can we go a little closer? I want to ask Ciara something," I asked, just as nervous as she and the others were.

Alzora hesitated before diving downward. "I don't know how your little insane mind thinks it's safe to go down there, but we are only staying for a second. If you want, we can plan out how to take down the big guy later..."

"Was that a hint of cowardice I heard in your voice?" I chuckled.

"As if! I bet that's not even a real word!" She argued diving quickly toward Ciara.

I could hear Asher yelling in the distance. "Just embrace the cowardly feelings, Alzora. That's what I do."

Ciara slowly walked toward the tip of the dragon's nostrils and laughed. "You really don't give up, do you? I thought I left it to Beckett to kill you, but I guess he failed. Should have figured he was good for nothing. Oh, have you met my little friend, Gedeon? He's a beauty, isn't he? I know for a fact that he will see to it that you all are destroyed. The poor little guy told me about how evil all the other dragons are. How dare they cast him to the lonely abyss of darkness? I can't understand how anyone wouldn't immediately fall in love with him."

"Little friend…that's an understatement. Ciara. Is that the weapon you mentioned? Why are you using a dragon to destroy all other dragons? I thought you hated them all, including him."

"Don't say such harsh things! Gedeon isn't like the others. He is very passionate about killing dragons. You're such a good boy, aren't you Gedeon? I would never abandon you like they would," she praised, rubbing his scales.

Gedeon released the pleased growl from his lips, and it sent vibrations through the sky. His eyes glimmered with a fiery glow, and he stared at us as he hovered in the air. Maybe I imagined things, but I thought I saw a small smile shift across his snout. What was he up to?

"Doesn't seem that way to me. Even if something like that happened in the past, how could any being who wants to take the life of others be good? Are you so afraid to fight me that you make your friends do it instead? I'm done fighting your lackeys. First Rolland, then Beckett, and now Gedeon. He will fall just like the others." I wasn't exactly sure what I was saying or why the words slipped from my mouth, but it felt like that needed to be said.

Ciara stood up straight and charged toward us, ready to leap off Gedeon's head. "How dare you say my Gedeon is not a good boy! You really want to fight me one on one? So be it!"

With a single leap, she was in the air only centimeters away from me. Before I realized what she was attempting to do, I felt a tug on my arm strong enough to tear me from Alzora. Ciara smiled as we plummeted to the rattling ground. Somehow, we managed to roll onto Gedeon's wing, and all the way down to the ground, but the landing was still painful. My leg was still in a great deal of pain, but I could at least bear it as I hopped backward. The flustered Alzora up above watched us, stunned. Only moments before she prepared to dive to get me, I shouted, "I'm ok down here! Go find a way to take down Gedeon. Hurry up!"

"How? And what do you mean you're fine? You're covered in scratches, and you can barely walk! You idiotic human!" Alzora argued back.

"I know you can figure something out. Just go already!"

Ciara tapped her foot in impatience and rolled her eyes. "Ok, Whisper? You wanted a fight? You got one. So, how about you focus a bit on me, for once. I'll even give you the first attack. See how nice I am?"

I shook my head in disagreement. "No. I'm not going to attack you. I want to talk. I want to convince you that you are wrong!"

"Well, that's too bad, I guess because whether you like it or not, I am going to kill you," she calmly stated as she pounced toward me at an incredible speed.

I guess it was stupid of me to think that I could just have a normal talk. Great. Maybe if I block her attacks, for now, I can manage to get a few words across to her. If possible, I really don't want to hurt her. I still refuse to believe that my whole friendship with her has been a lie.

I noticed that when she charged, her fist immediately became armored with thick black scales surrounded by the same dark mist surrounding Gedeon. That was definitely a new trick, and the only defense I could think of was an ice shield. I literally made a circular shield of ice. Talk about lack of imagination. I tucked my elbows into my sides as I tightly grasped the shield with both hands, embracing the powerful punch. The blow was powerful enough to push me back a couple of feet, but I held my stance.

"That's a handy trick, now isn't it?" She asked.

"What? My shield or your scaly fist?"

"Both, I guess. My precious Gedeon gave me this ability, making me invincible!" Ciara exclaimed as she ruthlessly punched the shield. The longer her rampage went on, the more pain I felt in both my chest and my injured leg.

"Dragons are graceful, amazing creatures. Why can't you understand that they mean no harm!" I yelled as I stepped forward.

She laughed and switched sides to attack once more. "You could never be more wrong! They are dangerous, horrible beings who think they can do whatever they want. Things would be better if they would all just die. On top of it all, they are selfish and annoying."

I looked up to the sky at Alzora and the others who were desperately launching their attacks at Gedeon, who didn't even feel a thing. They could have just fled and left me, along with all the other humans on this planet to die. But no, they are fighting. If that isn't selfless, then I don't know what is. As I endured her attacks, I drifted into my mind once more.

I honestly have no clue how they are going to take down Gedeon. It's not like we can use his size against him in any way, he is just too big. Alzora could try to freeze his legs to the ground, but there's no guarantee that he won't be able to get up from it. Wait, what is she doing?

Above me, Alzora had shifted into a spiraled dive onto Gedeon's body. Soon Zephyr and Ugi followed, each landing in a separate area. It was difficult to see from my position, but it looked like Alzora was going to each individual scale on Gedeon and freezing the sensitive mist-surrounded skin underneath. Ugi was doing a similar action, but instead, he was using his talons to shove through Gedeon's skin and electrocute his body. Somehow, Zephyr's flames were burning with such heat, that part of Gedeon's scale melted along with the burning flesh. Obviously, Gedeon was feeling these attacks, because his roar bellowed through the clouds. His scales might be impenetrable, but my friends found a way to break through them. Even Jaser and Asher were helping.

As Geodeon howled in pain, Ciara turned toward him. "Gedeon! Poor dear! Hurry up and take them before they cause you any more pain."

"What do you mean by that?" I worriedly asked.

Ciara smiled and glanced at me. "Oh, you'll see."

"No, I don't want to see!" I yelled.

Gedeon began to shake his body, and a black mist rose from beneath the scales on his body, rapidly engulfing him until he looked like he was only made up of the darkness itself. Alzora, Zephyr, and Asher managed to get away in time, but Ugi and Jaser were too late. When they rose from the mist, they spurted electricity everywhere, even toward the others. I understood everything now. Gedeon was the source of the controlling, hateful powers, and he finally had Ugi and Jaser in his grasp. I needed to warn the others, but I wasn't sure how they would stay away from the mist.

"Guys!" I yelled in the hope that my voice would reach them.

"Don't you dare interfere! Gedeon will control the others just like those two, and you can't do anything about it," she hissed.

She bounced back into her series of attacks, each harder than before. I did my best to hold up the shield, but I knew it was cracking with each attack. Even a glacier would snap against enough pressure.

They don't hear me. I need to let them know before it's too late, though! What do I do?

I turned to see the volcano exploding from the top, and it gave me an idea. A beacon. Maybe, just maybe, Alzora might understand. In that second, as the shield burst into a thousand pieces, I sent a bright beam of ice into the sky and wished for the best. My body flung backward with Ciara's punch. I couldn't roll over to dodge her shoe as it crushed my hand and pinned me to the ground. I held in my screams of agony and smiled at Ciara.

"What the heck are you smiling for, you stupid girl. You are so flawed compared to everything and everyone else in this world. I don't understand how you have even made it this far. You are such an inferior species! Give it up already. Accept your fate."

"Go ahead and judge me! Call out my faults, see if I care. All you will find are imperfections, and you know what, I don't mind! My faults are what make me who I am, and I'm not giving up. I won't back down, not until this Earth is saved."

What did she mean by inferior species? Isn't she human, too? I mean the way she's acting is inhuman, but she still is one of us.

Ciara rolled her eyes and stepped harder onto my hand. "Cut the crap. You are just delaying your demise even more."

I couldn't help but laugh. "Not exactly, I just needed time for this." Quickly, I threw my free hand into the air for Alzora to grab as she flew by. Carefully, I climbed up her arm onto her back and tossed two archway shaped pieces of ice toward Ciara's wrists, pinning her to the ground just like she did to me. I did the same with her legs and turned back toward the others as she screamed in frustration.

"Thanks. Ok, so you guys need to stay away from that mist. It's kind of like that mind-controlling device, but this stuff seeks destruction," I said.

"Well, how do we get rid of it?" Alzora asked, concerned.

"Can you and Zephyr try to combine your wing beats to blow it away?" I kept an eye on Ugi and Jaser as they annihilated everything in their path.

"We can try but what do we do about those dimwits?" Alzora glanced in my direction and then back at the others.

"Avoid them." I wasn't sure what else to say. I just knew we needed to stay away from that dangerous duo.

Zephyr appeared out of nowhere and chimed in. "Indeed, they seem to be more focused on random destruction than a specific target."

"That's a lot of mist, though. How do we know it will work?" Asher asked cautiously.

"I guess we won't know until we try." Alzora glanced at her wings for a minute, almost as if she doubted her abilities.

"Seems reasonable." Zephyr stretched his large wingspan, attempting to show off how superior he was.

"You ready, hothead?" Alzora asked passive-aggressively.

"I have been ready, you frozen worm." He smiled for a moment and fixed his eyes on the mist.

"Wow, even in a life or death situation you two still manage to argue." I facepalmed but watched as they positioned themselves next to the mist. "Ok, we need to take care of him after the mist leaves or else he will just make more. Can we try to attack the skin underneath his neck?"

"That may work as his weak point, but I am unsure how long it will take to stun him long enough to bring in a full attack," Zephyr stated.

Spreading their wings both Alzora and Zephyr synchronized their beats to create a powerful burst of wind. At first, it wasn't working but as they beat their wings faster and with more force the mist slowly fell off Gedeon's massive body, revealing the horror that shocked us all. His body had converted into the dark substance, and no matter how hard we tried, he remained in that terrifying state. He growled but did not seem to create more of the mind-manipulating mist. Slowly but surely, his skin and scales appeared once more, turning him back into his usual dragon state. I assumed it was because we blew enough away to prevent him from completing his transformation.

Now was our chance, our only chance. Immediately, we each dove toward his neck and landed. Gedeon shook his head from side to side, as we clung to his scales, attempting to either freeze them or catch them on fire. After about a minute, the attacks were affecting him. He was still just as frustrated, but he was slowing down. With all my power, I shoved both my hands under a scale and produced as much ice power as I could possibly make. Between the burns from both ice and fire, Gedeon was going downhill quick.

As we continued to attack, I heard a familiar voice from above. "Hello, down there. Need a little help?"

"Mikau! Vitus!" I yelled astonished. "What are you doing here? I thought you had no interest in this battle."

"Well, what's the use of saving the world from high taxes if there isn't a world to save at all," Mikau said as he smiled.

"I was also a little worried about your safety," Vitus added.

"Well, better late than never!" I waved them over.

As Vitus flew closer, he froze in midair and looked down confused. "This energy…"

"Hey, something wrong?" Mikau asked.

Vitus shook his headed and continued downward. "Something's not right… that thing…he isn't real."

That sentence had caught us all off guard, especially me. "What do you mean he isn't real, Vitus?"

"Indeed, what are you getting at? His attacks seem real to me," Zephyr asked.

"I mean, he isn't a dragon. At least not anymore. He is actually just materialized darkness."

"That doesn't make sense. How can darkness materialize?" Alzora asked, frustrated.

"How do you even know this?" Asher was beginning to panic.

Vitus explained. "I don't know…I just do? It's more of a feeling. Maybe it's just because I am a dragon made of the Earth's life energy, but I know it's true. The darkness…I can feel it. It is the combined sorrow, hatred, and confusion of one lonely dragon who faded from existence years ago. I can sense it all—the bloodlust from being betrayed by his family, and the pain of being orphaned until his only guidance was darkness. Why he has materialized, I do not know, but I know he will not be defeated easily."

"But he looks so real! Dudes, there's so much detail and everything!" Asher exclaimed, trying to fathom what was going on.

Mikau put some thought toward his next response. "Could that be because that was what he looked like before he died?"

Vitus smiled. "Bingo. That's my guess as well."

"Ok, so how do we beat him? I thought what we were doing before was weakening him, so was he just faking it?" Alzora continued to freeze Gedeon's scales to prevent any surprise attacks.

"Not necessarily. Gedeon believes he is in pain. Therefore, he is acting as expected. Since he is nothing more than darkness, he really isn't supposed to be feeling anything." The wind raced against Vitus's smooth snout as he spoke, blowing his shiny spinal feathers all over the place.

"Ok, but how do we beat him?" Alzora repeated once more.

Vitus squinted his eyes and peered down at Gedeon. "It's impossible...wait...if we can combine our powers into one single attack simultaneously, then maybe he will revert to his dark mist appearance one final time and fade away."

But would that really work? Why would he disappear just because he reverted to the mist? Last time he took that form, it looked as if he was as strong as ever. Even then we were lucky to prevent him from becoming that monster. Couldn't he just rematerialize? Vitus, what are you up to?

"But we already tried that. Plus, we don't have Ugi and Jaser on our side this time." Asher tilted his head in confusion.

"Let me take care of that." Vitus smiled and quickly flew over to the rampaging duo of destruction. The closer he drew, the more his feathers ruffled from the static. However, Vitus managed to dodge all the stray lightning bolts and catch up with them. He latched his talons onto Ugi's arm, and I watched as the electricity flowed through both Ugi and Jaser's body into Vitus, sending a very noticeable shock. Vitus closed his fried eyes for a minute, and a calming glow radiated from his scales and feathers. As he let him loose, Ugi shivered in the air and then looked around in absolute embarrassment.

"I'm sorry! I didn't mean to go crazy like that! I couldn't stop myself," Ugi apologized in a panic.

"I should probably be sorry, but that was actually really fun." Jaser couldn't help but sneak in a snicker.

"Don't worry, Gedeon was controlling you. We need your help now." Vitus shyly smiled and gently nudged Ugi's wing.

"How did you do that?" I was so relieved to see Ugi and Jaser back to normal. We had prevented a disaster. Correction. We had prevented more of a disaster. Our situation was bad as it was.

"Well, light conquers darkness after all. I just absorbed their hateful feelings and converted them into happy feelings." Vitus shrugged.

"That's a little weird, but good job?" Asher applauded as he smiled.

Vitus blushed. I didn't even know dragons could do that. "Thank you," he said politely.

"Enough chattering. To be blunt, I have had quite enough of this monstrosity. All in favor of taking care of him this instant?" Zephyr threw his wings open and ignited flames on both his wings and spine.

Asher's hand jumped in the sky excitedly out of nowhere. "I!"

"Hey... I second that!" Mikau smiled and joined him, kind of like it was a game.

"Doesn't that usually come after a motion?" I asked.

"Oh, whatever, I like it!" Mikau smiled, put his hands on his hips, and tilted his chin to the clouds, proud.

"Guys, can we get back to the point now," Alzora muttered, annoyed.

"Yeah, I want to kill something!" There was the crazy Jaser we all knew and loved.

"Are you sure you turned him back to normal?" Asher looked over at him and ducked behind Zephyrs twisted horns.

"Yes, I am afraid your little friend is just a psychopath." Vitus scratched his cheek with one talon and wore an uncertain grin.

"Even I could tell that, and I barely even met him. Still, he's my boy, Jaser!" Mikau exclaimed, as trusting as ever.

"Can we please stop Gedeon already? You know the Earth is still crumbling as we speak." I couldn't help but chuckle at their conversation because it was so true, but we needed to concentrate.

Ugi curled his wings into a dive to rejoin our group and flailed his talons around. "I thought we could stall a little longer. Gedeon is scary."

"Are you ready?" I asked in all seriousness, giving a glance to each one of them.

They nodded as we all gathered above Gedeon and circled in the smoky sky. "You will not destroy my home! Ready guys? Now!" I commanded, as if I was the general of an army.

The dragons all opened the mouths gathering as much energy and power possible, as we humans gathered a ball of power in our hands. On the signal, we released a beam of our combined powers at Gedeon's head. It was like a ray of beauty; it shined with more colors than the rainbow. It was unexplainable, but we didn't have time to focus on its beauty. If we wanted to take down Gedeon, we needed to pull through using as much energy possible. My body ached, and the more ice power I produced, the more exhausted I felt.

At last, Gedeon released a roar louder than ever and began to slowly turn into that black mist that had emitted from his body. We pushed through the pain and exhaustion until his whole body had converted into the mist of darkness once again. To our surprise, the mist just hovered there. The wind had no effect on it, and it didn't even bother to succumb to gravity. It stayed there as if frozen.

Vitus was the only one to speak, but he wore such a soft smile that made me worried. "I guess now is as good a time as any to tell you. The mist isn't going to go away. The darkness can't and will never disappear. Whether it be now or centuries from now, Gedeon won't stop until he has taken revenge. If it's not Gedeon, then it will just be another one of the darkness' puppets, but you don't have to worry. I will take care of it."

"What are you talking about, Vitus? You aren't planning to…because you can't…it will kill you!" Mikau shouted.

"It's ok, Mikau. You and the planet will be safe, and that's all that matters," he reassured Mikau calmly.

"I don't know what you're planning, but there has to be another way. We can just find a different way to destroy the mist! He is at his weakest. We could just keep attacking. There's no need for you to risk your life or anything," I stuttered, fearing what Vitus might do.

Clouds rolled in the sky forming an early tornado, but Vitus slowly shook his head and looked to the sky, ignoring every ounce of destruction around him. "Even if we found another way, it wouldn't save us. Gedeon had risen from the Earth's core. Sorry to say it, but this planet is going to die, either way, whether we truly destroy the darkness or not, the core is broken...unless you let me help you, we all will die."

"What does that mean? How could the core be damaged? I thought it was indestructible. There's a chance you can live through this, right? We can help you if it's that dangerous," Asher insisted.

"I'm afraid it doesn't work that way. Hey, but it's ok. I am a life dragon after all. Isn't this what I was called to do? This way I can allow Gedeon to make peace and finally leave this world." Vitus stretched his paw into the nearest cloud and held it like a delicate, fragile baby.

"You can't do this!" Mikau yelled as Vitus gently set him behind me on Alzora's back and flew toward the cloud of pitch-black mist. His feathered tail writhed behind him in the treacherous wind as he soared downwards.

Vitus smiled once more, and closed his eyes, slowly absorbing all of the dark mist. As the mist depleted more and more, Vitus's feathers that once shined so bright and colorful, turned dim and dull. Through the process, I could barely hear him speak to Gedeon. "Life is strange, isn't it? Both you and I were cast away from our rightful village. Somehow, fate sent me to Mikau, such a wonderful boy, and guided me to be the dragon I am today. You, on the other hand, were cast out in the same way, alone and afraid. It's sad. One destined to obey darkness and another destined to consume and convert it to light. The unwritten destiny. The twisted legends of fate have intertwined.

Those legends of the past do not matter anymore. Don't worry Gedeon. You will be free of his control soon enough. We will be free, free of the pain that bound us for so long. It makes me so happy. I wish you could have gotten to know the humans. They are truly amazing…" He used the last of his energy to glide down to the ground and grip the dying soil with all his might. Vitus emitted a glow brighter than ever, a light that quelled the shaking, slumbered the volcano and sewed the ravines.

"See y-you're fine," Mikau stuttered in a worried laugh, knowing he was lying to himself.

"Yes, I am fine now that I know the planet is safe," Vitus's tail twitched and his feathers fell as he lay alone on the warm dirt.

Alzora, Ugi, and Zephyr held their heads down clenching their teeth while Asher and I sobbed. One by one, tiny light particles appeared around Vitus, rising to the sky. He didn't seem to mind as he held up his paws and sat on his hind legs, peering at the essence escaping from within. Mikau rushed to his side, pressing Vitus's head against his own. Though Vitus smiled, there was an unmistakable sorrow in his eyes.

"Now promise me something, ok? I saved the physical world. Now you need to go and save it from those high taxes." Vitus said as he patted Mikau on the head.

"No! What's the point now? I wanted to do it with you…but now…but now…" Mikau argued in more sorrow than anger.

"But now it's time for me to say goodbye. It'll be alright. Don't stop pursuing your dreams because of me." More and more light particles began to rise from Vitus's while body and the more that went, the faster the others appeared.

Mikau was begging at this point while he tugged on Vitus's arm. "It's not fair! You're my friend…my best friend. Please don't go."

"I know. You are mine, as well. My own kind abandoned me since birth, but you have stayed by my side since the very beginning, and I will never forget that. I am so lucky to have met all of you as well. You are all such great people and dragons. I'm happy to call you all my friends." Vitus yawned and looked around. "I know the Earth, our home, will be safe in your hands."

"Vitus don't go! We just met, and it's not fair for you to sacrifice your life for us!" I screamed, fighting back the tears as they rushed down my face.

"You know he has no choice," Alzora added still looking toward the ground in grievance.

"She's correct. If Vitus does not do this, we all will indeed die, just as Gedeon did so long ago." Zephyr bowed his head in respect.

"And…and he will sacrifice himself as a hero," Ugi spoke through his sobs.

"But…but…" I tried to argue against it, but my tears were overwhelming.

The particles sped up in a circular motion around Vitus until, at last, his body began to fade into transparency. "Please don't be sad. I think it's time for me to go now…Mikau, you are such an amazing, talented boy. All I ask is that you remember me and remain your happy, funny self. Thank you…for everything."

Vitus smiled for the last time as the last of him faded from existence. The light particles that remained fell to the ground and sunk in below. It wasn't possible for me to focus on anything else. Vitus had sacrificed himself for the world, and we didn't even see it coming. Together the dragons bellowed their roar of both sorrow and respect into the skies in harmony. Vitus was gone. It may have just been my imagination, but as the last of Vitus faded away, I could hear a deep voice saying thank you, echo through the sky, almost synchronizing with Vitus's. Perhaps Gedeon was finally free, and maybe, just maybe the darkness was as well.

Chapter 14

Adjusting

All of us felt deep sorrow for Vitus's sacrifice, but what changed in our surroundings was a miracle. The lava roaming through the land faded away, the cracks in the ground sealed and turned into a bright green meadow, flowers of all colors sprouted for miles and miles, the clouds fled the dusk sky, the wind turned to a calm breeze, and a tree shot up into the sky where the O.S.I headquarters had previously crumbled. The tree itself had replaced the building rubble, and its trunk alone was as round, stretching 40 feet long in diameter. White flowers surrounded the base of the tree, and vines covered a section of the tree like a door.

The cuffs that bound Ciara to the ground faded away, and she slept with a peaceful smile after fading into unconsciousness. Beckett continued to sleep, but I wasn't sure whether it was because I knocked him out or if he was just tired. Birds chirped in the sky, and the wind passed. Time was passing for everything but us. We were frozen in the past. With tears still welling in his eyes, Mikau stood and walked over to the tree.

"Mikau?" I sniffled. "Where are you going?"

There was no answer, but I watched as he carefully walked through the vines on the base of the tree. I didn't even notice that there was an entrance for him to walk through. Was the tree hollow?

He's been in there for quite a bit now. I wonder if he's ok. Actually, he's not ok. His best friend just died. Still though, what is in there? Why Vitus? Leaving us here to grieve over your death. I know you said not to be sad, but that's not an easy task. We had fun together, even if it was for a short time.

At last, Mikau walked out of the tree with a sad smile, holding what looked to be an egg. The entrance to the tree sealed behind him, but he didn't even notice. Mikau continued to carefully walk toward us, staring at the precious egg in his hands. As he came closer, I recognized that the egg was a white and yellow scaled dragon egg. Unexpectedly, the egg wiggled, and tiny cracks appeared on the top. We gazed in awe.

As we huddled in a circle around the cracking egg, we held our breath in curiosity. First, a feathered tail poked out of the egg and then two tiny arms and legs. The tiny dragon used his mini feathered wings to break away the rest of the shell, leaving just a small piece left on top of his snout.

"Here you go little guy," Mikau spoke softly as he picked off the shell covering the little dragon's head.

The small, newly hatched dragon resembled Vitus, except he was golden and white and had even more feathers on him. The little dragon sneezed and peered at us with his huge crystal blue eyes.

"I see, so that was Vitus's plan," Zephyr said calmly.

Asher hopped off Zephyr's back and scratched the baby dragon's neck. "I don't get it. Dude, he is so cute!"

Zephyr turned his head, annoyed by his change in attitude. "Vitus saved a small amount of his life essence to reincarnate a version of himself."

"So, he's like a mini Vitus?" I smiled as I wiped the tears from my eyes and let out a small giggle. "Welcome back, Vitus."

Jaser jumped down as well and tilted his head in curiosity toward mini Vitus. "So, can all dragons do this?"

Alzora brushed her nose against the tiny dragon and smiled. "Not really, but there have been rare cases where a dragon with special abilities uses the last of their energy to recreate themselves. I wouldn't be surprised if this little guy acts just like Vitus. Of course, he won't have any memories of his past life, but he will make new ones with new friends."

Ugi stepped forward and shyly gave his opinion. "But where will he go? Vitus was originally banished like me for being different, so why would Pulri accept him now?"

"Ugi is correct. Vitus can't stay with the dragons, not if he wants to grow up living a happy life. Even if the elders did change their ways, the poor thing would grow up being looked down upon." Zephyr added.

I couldn't help but jump in. "Well, why can't Mikau raise him?"

"A human raising a dragon? It's unheard of." Alzora was stunned by my idea.

"Please let me keep him. I can take care of him. I was with Vitus long enough to learn what he likes and dislikes. He will be safe with me," Mikau insisted.

"We may not have any other choice. If you truly feel up to the task, then that is up to you." Zephyr pointed his snout toward the clear sky in the superior way he usually did.

"Just know that dragons grow extremely quickly, and we can have quite the temper. Well, not me, but most dragons," Ugi whispered to us humans.

I bit my lips trying not to laugh as I pointed at Alzora and Zephyr, who were giving each other deadly stares.

Mikau chuckled and held mini Vitus in his arms. The little dragon had fallen asleep. "Don't worry. I will take good care of him."

"Well do you at least need a ride back to your home?" Ugi knelt, waited for Jaser to hop back on his shell and then signaled Mikau over.

"I would appreciate that. Thank you," Mikau said softly as he climbed onto Ugi's shell behind Jaser.

"Oh? Are we leaving already?" I asked as I pulled myself onto Alzora's back.

"I miss Vitus," Asher mumbled as he slowly crawled onto Zephyr.

Before we took off, Alzora grabbed Ciara and set her next to me using her highly maneuverable tail. Zephyr did the same with Beckett.

Each of the dragons carefully drew back their wings and rose into the calm sky. I was the only one to look back at the peaceful land that was once plagued with chaos. It had been a long while since I had felt the gentle breeze of the wind. It was finally over. We'd saved the planet, and we all could finally rest. As we glided to Mikau's home, I stared at the scattered small clouds, dazed. It was hard to believe that our adventure was finally over.

Upon arrival at Mikau's home, Ugi was the only one to land while the rest of us hovered in the sky. As Mikau gently slid off Ugi's shell onto the lush grass below him, I smiled and waved. "Make sure you take care of baby Vitus, ok?"

Mikau put his fingers to his lips and smiled back. "He's in good hands. Don't forget, I still have to save this world from high taxes, so this isn't the last you will see of me."

"Well, I sure hope not." I laughed as Ugi hopped back into the air and joined our group.

We finally waved our last goodbye and flew into the orange sunset sky once more. "So where to now?" I asked out of curiosity.

Alzora glanced back at me, unsure of what to say. "Your home. That goes for both of you, actually. Jaser and Ugi are already on their own program so they can do whatever they like, but we must drop you guys back home."

"What, why?" Ok, so I had to admit to myself that the question was pretty dumb, but I didn't feel like I needed to leave them just yet.

Zephyr stopped to explain. "Our mission is finished. Therefore, we don't need you bothersome humans with us anymore."

"Well, that was mean," Asher mumbled poking the back of Zephyr's head.

Alzora paused and then turned her direction westward. "Mean or not, it's the truth. Fire scales, I guess I will see you back at the new dragon village."

"Agreed, see you then."

"Alright Jaser, I guess we should get going, too." Ugi sadly mumbled as he turned the other direction.

Each of us flew in opposite directions, and I didn't have the energy to argue. The flight lasted through the night into late the next day, and we were silent.

I mean, I get it. I don't want to be that one clingy person, but still, I will miss them. Even if they did let me stay, I would be surrounded by a bunch of potentially dangerous dragons who could care less about me. At least, I get to go home to a family. Poor Asher

has no one. He is just going to go back to his little house in New
Zealand with his kiwis and hermit crab.

We arrived at my house at midnight, and luckily, my window was still unlocked, making an easy entrance. I stepped off Alzora blindly because of how dark it was. "You sure Ciara can stay at your house with no trouble?" she asked.

"Well, I can just chain her down like before if it gets out of hand. She has nothing, not even Gedeon's power, so I think she'll be fine. Thank you for everything, Alzora," I said as I picked up Ciara and held her with both hands.

I heard a faint, "Yeah. Be good little human," then I felt a small gust of wind. I turned around only to see the dim light post flicker and dust swirl into the air. Alzora had left just as quickly as she had arrived.

I put on a rueful grin and shook my head. "How did I know she was going to do that?"

I set Ciara down for a moment so I could open the window to my room. Carefully, I lifted her up and over onto an empty beanbag chair. Once I entered, I locked the window, turned on the light, and looked around my clean room. It seemed so small compared to everything I had been through. Though I was exhausted, I took a quick ten-minute shower and returned to my room in my warm pajamas. It felt nice to be clean again, but I was still sad. I missed my friends.

Oh, right. Ciara should be waking up soon. I forgot that I gave her medicine to make her stay sleep the whole flight here. I wonder if she is going to try to kill me again when she wakes up. That could be problematic.

I sat on my bed and stared at her. I didn't know what to think or even say. Was she still my friend? Did she truly hate me? All I could think to do was hug her, but I didn't expect her arms to wrap around me and hug back. Ciara had finally woken up, and I had no clue what to say. I just stared at her blankly.

"Where am I? Are we having a sleepover?" she asked with a clueless expression.

Doesn't she remember? She couldn't have forgotten everything that happened? Right? Is that even possible? Maybe I can play along. I guess I can see if she remembers the dragons.

"Yeah, that's exactly what's happening. What's the last thing you remember doing, like what did you do yesterday?" I asked, a little too seriously.

"Well, that's a silly thing to ask. Hm, let's see. Oh right! I just got back from my family vacation," she recalled excitedly.

"Oh, I remember you saying that you were going on some kind of trip. I bet it was fun. Did you hang out with any dragons?" I tried to ask without sounding too weird.

"It was really fun! Oh, come on," she giggled, oblivious to the real situation, "you are the only one crazy enough to believe in those creatures."

She really doesn't remember anything. I guess it's for the best, though. She still thinks she just finished high school and that dragons don't exist. Good. She will be safer that way. I just have to play dumb.

I laughed a little at her comment and tossed her the remote to my T.V. "Yeah. Well, something tells me that you aren't planning on sleeping any time soon. I'm sorry to do this to you, but I'm tired and need a little sleep."

"No worries! I'll keep it on low volume, so I don't wake you up. Goodnight!" she said happily.

I didn't even bother to turn off the light or reply to her. I was so tired that I immediately fell into my dreams. The next morning, I walked Ciara home and took a walk by myself for a while, pondering life. I assumed that Beckett had gone back to Pulri with his memory of the whole ordeal erased as well. Both Beckett and Ciara were just Gedeon's pawns to take over the world and were used as an attempt to stop us before we came too close. I was almost certain that Beckett was relieved to get home and be reunited with Dympna, his little furry companion.

I was utterly bored for the next few days. I tried to pass the time by playing on my laptop, watching T.V., and hanging with Ciara, but nothing changed the way I felt. Sorrow filled a section of my heart. As weeks passed, part of me began to question if my whole adventure was just a dream that I couldn't wake up from.

Some days, I would drive myself over to the place where I first met Alzora, or shall I say the place where she kidnapped me. Often, I would peer over the town with a blank mind and think about the fun times we all had. Weeks turned to months, and I was beginning to feel like coming to the rocky mountains was hopeless.

Am I ever going to see them again? Alzora. Asher. Zephyr. Ugi. Jaser. Even Mikau and baby Vitus. I miss all of them so much. I miss Alzora and Zephyr's bickering, Ugi's stuttered apologies and paranoid complaints, Asher's nerdy video game talk, and Jaser's insane threats. I can't help but miss everything about every one of them. We didn't even leave with a goodbye. We just up and left. How am I supposed to live in a world without you guys?

I couldn't help but begin to talk to myself. "How could you just leave me like that? Seriously, I know you guys can be mean at times, but that was just cruel."

"Oh, come now! I don't think it was cruel, whatsoever. After all, we convinced Pulri to let us explore the world doing whatever we please. What pleases me is to have a human by my side. So, Whisper, will you be my rider again?" I knew that voice.

I knew it so well that I frantically turned around and wrapped my arms tightly around Alzora's neck. "You meanic! Of course, I will! I missed you so much! Wait, you said we. Does that mean…"

224

"Hi!" Asher yelled from atop of the smug, smiling Zephyr.

"What's up? Long time no see," Jaser greeted, raising one hand.

"But why? I thought you liked living with the other dragons." My eyes almost burst with tears of joy.

"Too boring. I forgot my life kind of sucks." Alzora shrugged.

"Those foolish weaklings. They didn't even acknowledge that we helped save the planet from destruction, either," Zephyr proclaimed.

It was nice to know that Zephyr didn't just feel superior to humans. He acted superior to literally every being he met. We had somehow managed to bring ourselves back together once again. I quickly climbed up Alzora's back, and we rose into the never-ending sky, looking forward to the adventure that awaits ahead.

Some people may see dragons as treasure-hoarding, fire-breathing beasts, but my friends and I know otherwise. Our dream is to explore the world—maybe fight some crime if we get the chance—with our quick-tempered, kind-hearted, loving friends in search of the rest of the missing dragons. That legend about us destroying everything in sight turned to ash just as Gedeon reverted to mist. So, here we are now, the destined ones. This time we are destined for much, much more—destined for adventure.

A Note From An Ice Pair

Dear Reader,

I hope you enjoyed listening to my story! I had so much fun on this trip, even if we were almost killed a couple times. I am so happy that things turned out this way. Life is way more exciting when you can live it out to the fullest and serve justice to some bad guys along the way. I wish I could continue to write a little longer, but you know who is trying to steal the pen.

Greetings, tiny humans! I hope you all aren't as, well...annoying? Persistent? No, as willful and determined as Whissper is—is that how she spells her name? Whatever, I don't care, where was I? She caused so much trouble and chaos on this trip, but if I must say...she ended up being helpful. To say the least, this has definitely been an exciting and entertaining trip. I think you have heard enough about me. Whether she likes it or not, I'm closing this letter and mailing it right now. Be good my human friends, and live life to the fullest.

Sincerely,

Whisper and Alzora

The Memo From Fire

Dear Incompetent Humans,

I have one question, and one alone, for you. How do you write with these tiny pens? They do not fit in my talons properly. Oh, I suppose I should give my opinion on our little mission. Well, I have never traveled with a more idiotic group in my life. The nagging and annoyance were overwhelming...but, if I must be truthful, I admire the kind and brave hearts that they hold deep within. I could go on forever writing about my superiority and handsomeness, but alas, my dear friend would like to say something.

I think Whisper's letter idea was amazing! Hi, so I'm Asher, but I guess you already knew that! Sorry for hiding the fact that I'm a hacker, I just wasn't sure how to tell everyone. So, my dudes, if you ever need a hacker just let me know. This adventure has been so fun, and better yet I made so many new friends. Ok, my dudes, I have to go. Zephyr just accidentally set Jaser on fire. At least I hope it was an accident. Just know this, if you smile, you will be happy, so be optimistic and put on a big smile. Smile because life is spectacular and so are you. Stay happy, smile, and never stop moving forward.

Faithfully yours,

Asher and Zephyr

Does This Really Need A Title?

Dear Human Friends,

Hello! Ugi speaking, well writing, but you know what I mean. This mission changed my life! I still can't believe I gained so many new friends. Is that bad? Sorry! I still have to keep a close eye on Jaser, or else he may make a mess that even I can't clean up; that boy will give me a heart attack! Oh right, the letter. I don't really know what to say, but Jaser won't stop yanking my tail so I will hand the paper to him. Hopefully, you will receive it in one piece.

Why am I writing on a stupid scrap of paper? Alright, opinion...yeah. It was fun. After all, I did get to bash some heads in. Plus, I heard we get to catch even more people in our next mission; I can't wait to listen to their screams. Chicken and I can combine our lightning now, so that's pretty cool. Let's see what else to say. I hang out with Asher quite a bit, even though Whisper thinks I am a bad influence on him, whatever that means. She can be such a drag sometimes, but at least she is good competition for everything we do together. Ok, I'm bored, so here's the last of my message. Carlosi, Sharonis, thanks for hanging with me when I needed some help. Oh, and thanks for the grub. Sorry I attacked the restaurant owner.

P.s. I had nothing against him, I just felt like it.

Regards,

Jaser and Ugi

I am still here, I cannot be vanquished. I am darkness itself. No matter how many of my pawns you may defeat, I will forever come after you, for this is my world. I linger in each of your hearts, and you can never throw me away. How long will this petty battle between light and darkness continue? Accept your fate, I will not die.

Visit the Legends Turned to Ash Facebook page for more information

www.ingramcontent.com/pod-product-compliance
Lightning Source LLC
Chambersburg PA
CBHW031723170626
46808CB00005B/1861